CANE'S LANDING

BY PATRICK HENNESSY

7/2/2017

to Vicky & Rob —

thanks for the

encouragement —

Enjoy

Pat

Painting By: Holli Hennessy

Photo By: Chris Overcash
www.overcashphotography.com

PREAMBLE

This is the third and final book in the *Cane's Landing* series. I tried to write each book to stand alone, but I know the books make more sense if read as a series. I made up the characters and the events. None of the characters exists, but some of the places do exist and the Cane name was chosen from history.

Many locals know that Cane's Landing was a port for the Elysian Groves Plantation located where Bossier City, Louisiana later grew into a city. The plantation was owned and run by Mary Cane. As a child I remember being told that there was a ford in the Red River near Cane's landing. That memory is probably flawed since my recent research reveals that steamboats used the port. A trail and ferry apparently did traverse the river near Cane's Landing.

When we moved to Bossier City, there was a two lane bridge with a curve in it between Shreveport and Bossier City. I remember the bridge being called the Traffic Street Bridge. I always thought or assumed that the Bossier side of the bridge would have terminated in the area of Cane's Landing. That bridge was torn down in the early 60's to make room for the I-20 Bridge.

I also use the Long Allen-Bridge, known locally as the Texas Street Bridge in the book. In the book the Texas Street Bridge is the Neon Bridge which was first lit in 1993, and sadly no longer shines. The photo on the back cover of the book was taken by Chris Overcash in 2007.

The book is not about Cane's Landing, the place, nor is it about country music; even though I again used the titles to country songs as chapter titles. In most cases, the songs were recorded by artists who appeared on the Louisiana Hayride. I have listed the songs with short comments in an appendix at the end of the book. I hope you can listen to the songs as you read the book.

CHAPTER 1. *BLOODY MARY MORNING.* Willie Nelson

https://www.youtube.com/watch?v=DQWCPbxcA1I

It was not every day that James "Jake" Cane had an opportunity to ride in a Gulfstream jet. In fact, Jake had never before been on such an airplane. Likewise, it was not every day that he flew on a jet with the husband of a woman he had spent the last days with on a tropical island. Jake could not shake the thought, a *fool again, not just a fool, but a used fool.*

Jake was not particularly comfortable with any of this. Still, he attempted to pay attention and understand Stanley's explanation of why he had run off with a gay lover and the reasons why he had come back to his wife and so easily forgiven her for the affair with Jake. Given the sensual beauty of his wife, Stanley told Jake he totally understood Jake's behavior and held no ill will. Jake had time, between his other thoughts and worries, to conclude that he would not feel the same way if it were his wife who had been a willing originator of the activities of the last several days.

For her part, Stanley's wife, Natalia, obviously satisfied that her plan had come together, spent much of the trip contently sleeping. At best, it was an awkward and uncomfortable situation. As Jake sipped on a Bloody Mary expertly prepared by the handsome, even pretty, young man Stanley referred to as the steward, he wondered, *did Stanley really think that he, Jake and Natalia could ever be real friends?*

Jake had accepted the free trip home from St. Thomas, U.S.V.I., for one reason, and the reason was not to make up with his "friend" Stanley Joe Coleman, III.

No, there were other reasons and they did not include either of the Colemans. For one thing, Jake had wanted to reconcile with his wife from the day she threw him out for a good and valid reason, an affair with a secretary in his office. He had at last been asked by his wife to return home, but it was unlikely that the invitation was as a result of her forgiveness. There were other more obvious reasons. Jake's unmarried, college-student daughter was pregnant and even more disturbingly, Jake's wife, Jen, was also pregnant. With his own such personal problems, it was next to impossible for Jake to concentrate on Stanley's heart to heart.

The additional reason for Jake's distraction was even more troubling: Jubilee Jones. Jake had never met Jubilee Jones, and hoped that he never would. Jubilee Jones was the chief FBI agent in the Memphis office, and Jake knew that he was investigating the murder of the brother of a U. S. Senator in the aftermath of Hurricane Katrina. The fact that Jubilee wanted to talk to Jake could not be a good thing. Jake was not involved at all in the murder of the Senator's brother, but Jubilee had the notion that there was a connection between the murder and an earlier shootout in Brownsville, Tennessee. Jake did know something about the Brownsville shootings.

While estranged from his wife, Jake had innocently witnessed a drug deal in Brownsville that had evolved into a deadly shootout. After witnessing the participants in the drug deal shoot each other, Jake had made the decision to help himself to the drugs and money left lying among the melee. Jake wanted to believe that he would not have made the same decision had he been living happily with his wife. Whatever the reason for the decision, it had been a decision that changed Jake's life: a decision that had thrust Jake, a successful businessman and admired civic leader, into another world; a decision that had led to two killings and a murder all involving Jake; a decision that left Jake in possession of over $1,000,000 in dirty drug money. Money from which Jake could not free himself, notwithstanding the fact that Jake did not need nor want the money.

The actual reason Jake had accepted the ride with Stanley was based on his correct conclusion: Jubilee Jones would be meeting his Delta flight scheduled to arrive in Shreveport, Louisiana from Atlanta some five hours after Jake would actually arrive on Stanley's Gulfstream. The cushion would allow Jake time to talk to his wife and more importantly, time to talk to his best friend, Buddy Hawkins. Jake was in trouble, trouble like he had never seen. Normally, Buddy would provide answers for the problems, but normally Buddy would not himself be in the middle.

For these reasons, at 37,000 feet over the Gulf of Mexico, as Stanley poured out his heart, it was challenging for Jake to listen. How had Jubilee found out about Jake? How much did Jubilee know? How could he know anything? What had Jen said to Jubilee? Did Jubilee know about Buddy? And, every once in a while, another thought crept in: *was he the father of Jen's unborn child*? How could his one sexual encounter with Jen in over a year have resulted in her pregnancy? Hardly any time was spent on arguably the most important problem – his unmarried, pregnant daughter.

CHAPTER 2. *HE'S A GOOD OLE BOY.*
Goldie Hill

https://www.youtube.com/watch?v=HkhQN9xZv0Y

It's complicated. Sidney Jones is a psychopath and is, coincidentally, the first cousin of Jubilee Jones. Sidney goes by the nickname, Pinky. Pinky worked for Robert Daniel Stephens, known to all as "Big D." Big D was the owner of D-Line Construction and a gentleman's club in Memphis called Platinum Plus. Both businesses were fronts for big D's most profitable occupation as a drug dealer. The money Jake now possessed had belonged to Big D, and, as it turns out, a heretofore, silent partner.

Jake and mostly Buddy, had made plans to return the money, but while Jake was attempting to return the money, Big D tried to kill Jake. Big D failed. Not only did he fail to kill Jake, but in the process was himself mysteriously and fatally shot. The attempted return and Big D's death occurred on Bourbon Street in New Orleans on the eve of Hurricane Katrina, and Pinky, there to support Big D, was stranded in New Orleans.

It gets more complicated. Pinky was bored, hot and dirty, so he shot the Senator's brother and stole the brother's Land Rover. He also took nearly everything else of value that would fit in the vehicle as well as one of the dogs the Senator's brother had unsuccessfully kept for protection. Pinky then maneuvered the Land Rover through the hurricane debris and escaped New Orleans.

A murder in New Orleans is not a federal crime, but the U. S. Senate is a small and powerful club, which is how Special Agent Jubilee Jones was assigned to investigate the murder.

When things got hot for Pinky, he disappeared using an alias concocted by Big D before he died. Pinky now goes by Manuel Guerra, and he has a bank account, a driver's license, credit cards, and even a vehicle titled in that name.

When Pinky, posing as Guerra, failed and almost got himself killed trying to get Big D's money from Jake and Buddy, he promised to disappear using the Guerra alias. Before they let Pinky leave, Buddy had equipped Pinky's truck and cell phone with tracking devices. For the preceding several weeks, Pinky had been living in south Dallas.

The alias Pinky was using had two serious flaws; Pinky was not Hispanic and he did not speak Spanish. There was another problem, the work available to a Hispanic was long, hard physical labor. Pinky was not cut out for such. Pinky preferred easier money, so he robbed his employer and left Dallas with the money and the Doberman Pincher he had acquired in the process of robbing the Senator's brother.

Pinky decided that he would go see an old girlfriend in Saginaw, Michigan, a woman Pinky had met while stuck in New Orleans after Hurricane Katrina, someone he had nicknamed "Ms. Saginaw." Being a psychopath, it never occurred to Pinky that he would not be welcomed by a woman he had robbed and left drunk, dirty, and penniless at Harry's Corner Bar when he left New Orleans. It certainly never crossed his mind that Ms. Saginaw would have the number to the local FBI office and instructions to call that number if she should be contacted by Pinky.

While passing through St. Louis on his way to Saginaw, the signal from the tracking device embedded in Pinky's truck was picked up by one of Buddy's old Army friends. The man was retired and had nothing better to do and nothing he would rather do than track Pinky. The man's instructions were to track Pinky at a safe distance and to report, in code, to Buddy. The man did not know why he was shadowing Pinky, and he did not ask.

Pinky had named the dog "Spike." Spike like Pinky was loyal to no one. Spike stayed with Pinky because it was convenient and most of all because Pinky fed him.

For their part, Buddy and Jake possessed neither knowledge of Ms. Saginaw nor any idea of why Pinky was in Michigan.

Back in Shreveport, Buddy wanted to remind Jake that they should have killed Pinky when they had the chance, all the while remembering that neither of them was in favor of the killing at the time.

Pinky had arrived in Saginaw at about the same time that Jake and Natalia arrived in St. John.

CHAPTER 3. *DON'T MESS WITH MY TOOT TOOT.* Doug Kershaw

https://www.youtube.com/watch?v=k3kLT-sK9YU

Jake stopped by Buddy's shop on the way home. He was torn between the desire to see his wife, Jen, and his need to report to Buddy. There was, of course, the lingering fear that Jen was only asking him back out of what she saw, through her Roman Catholic guilt, as duty to her unborn child and unborn grandchild. Jake was certain that she had neither forgotten nor forgiven. Jake knew that he would receive a warm reception from Buddy. You can't make old friends. He really did not know what to expect from Jen.

Buddy was working on a motorcycle in the shop when Jake arrived. Buddy only worked on cars and motorcycles for a select few. An old army injury and a more recent oil field injury made it difficult for Buddy to walk. Jake had not called ahead. Buddy had specifically instructed Jake that he should avoid all phone conversations for fear that Jake's phone was or would be bugged.

Buddy spoke first. "I found Pinky, and he's in Saginaw, Michigan. Do you have any idea why he would be in Saginaw, Michigan?"

"No, Buddy, no idea at all. Is someone following him?"

Buddy quickly filled Jake in on what he knew. "Yes, a friend of mine from the service. He lives in St. Louis. He is retired and happy to have something that gets him out of the house. There will be some expenses. Pinky must have suspected something. He threw his cell phone into a ditch in Dallas before he left. I guess we did a good job of hiding the bug in his pickup. So far, my man has nothing for us. The truck has been parked in a neighborhood for several days. It may be abandoned. My friend is getting a feeling that all is not as it appears. He's keeping his distance."

Jake dropped the bomb. "Has Jubilee Jones been by to see you?" Jake knew that it was unlikely that Buddy would have answered a call on his house phone, even from someone he knew. To talk to Buddy would require Jubilee to make a trip to Buddy's shop.

Buddy looked surprised. "What makes you ask?"

Jake was wishing that he had never involved Buddy in this huge mess. "Jubilee has contacted Jen. He wants to talk to me. I don't know anything about how he learned my name, and I don't know what, if anything, Jen has told him. I haven't been home yet, and I was not about to talk to Jen about any of this on the phone."

Most people would exhibit some concern with the fact that the FBI was looking into a situation in which they had some involvement with murder and dirty drug money. Not Buddy. Where most people would be worried sick, the news had the opposite effect on Buddy. No, Buddy's entire countenance seemed to light up. Buddy was energized by the news. Jake could see and feel it.

Buddy was thinking. "When you get home, ask Jen to call Clear Signal Phone Service. Tell them that she is hearing a buzz on the line. Ask them to come out and check the lines. We'll find out if the phones are bugged and we will know if they are bugged in the future." Buddy continued, "Innocently call Jubilee from your office. Tell him nothing. When you find out he is from the FBI, tell him you will need to call corporate counsel before you can talk to him. Act like you think it has something to do with stock trading. I bet you can find instructions in your employment manual that will back you up."

Buddy was correct. There was a section in the employment manual that dealt specifically with how a broker should handle a call from any government agency. Call corporate counsel. *How did Buddy know that?* Jake had already decided that they would also visit their lawyer, Timothy Barnette. Jake did not know that Jen had already visited with Tim. "I am going to see Tim, too. Do you think I should?"

Buddy answered. "When the FBI calls, any prudent man with sufficient money will call his lawyer. Jubilee will tell you it is unnecessary, but he will not be surprised when you do it anyway. You need a lawyer. Call him. I would not depend on some silk stocking corporate lawyer provided by your employer."

Jake wondered if Buddy would follow his own advice.

Jake was leaving when Buddy got a call. Buddy turned to Jake, "Wait, this is a call from Saginaw." Jake waited and listened to one side of the conversation. From the words spoken, Jake neither learned nor understood anything. The discussion appeared to be between the two men talking about a dove hunt. When the conversation was over, Buddy had some disturbing news, "Pinky was arrested by the FBI two days ago. They have just towed off his truck. It's a good thing that my friend kept his distance. He thinks that the FBI was watching the truck to see if Pinky had any accomplices. I told him to turn off and dispose of the tracking device."

Jake was thinking, *do you think Jones got my name from Pinky?*

Buddy was ahead of him. He knew exactly what Jake was thinking. "That's a good guess. Pinky is in deep shit, lethal injection type shit. I bet he is singing for his life."

Jake offered. "Pinky doesn't know who you are."

Buddy should have been concerned, maybe even angry, but he showed no concern. "Jake, we look enough alike to be twin brothers, how long do you think it will take for the FBI to come calling?"

Jake did not respond. There was nothing to say.

CHAPTER 4. *TIGER WOMAN.*
Claude King

https://www.youtube.com/watch?v=6xbmgKRiRC8

Danielle Stephens Gentry was sitting in her father's office, in his big leather chair, truly feeling sad about her father's death, but more so, sorry for herself. Danielle was Big D's only child, spoiled and sheltered. Danielle would need to grow up fast. Danielle was actually pretty, like her mother, but she was big like her father. Danielle had fought her weight for her entire life. She had been at her lowest weight for her marriage a little over a year ago, but was now at her highest.

She didn't care much for her husband Danny Gentry, who, as it turned out had married her for her money. Danny spent his time "managing" her father's gentleman's club, Platinum Plus. He was good looking, outgoing, irresponsible, and dumb. Danny got by on his looks and his family. Danielle's mother, a prescription drug addict, pressed her daughter to marry Danny mainly because he was from a good family. As it turned out, a "good" family that once had money. A "good" family that now had no money.

Danielle was intelligent like her father and although she did not yet know it she could, like her father, be shrewd and downright vicious. Harvey Nelson, the comptroller for D-Line Construction, sat across the desk from Danielle. Harvey was a small, balding, mousy man. He was not stupid, but he survived by being careful to ask and see little. Harvey knew a lot that no one could ever force him to admit. Danielle had been looking at the books and had discovered cash deposits into various projects, large cash deposits that turned what looked like a losing project into a profitable one. She also noticed subcontractors and suppliers who appeared to have never received payment for their work.

"Harvey, where do these cash deposits come from? Why do our customers pay with cash? Don't they need better proof of payment?" Danielle was bewildered, naïve.

Danielle would not get any answers from Harvey. "Danielle, you knew your dad. I never asked such questions. I just did what I was told."

Danielle persisted. "What about these subcontractors and suppliers who have not been paid? Why aren't they demanding payment?"

Harvey had no answers. As Harvey stood to leave the office, a swarthy man in a maroon shirt, pointy-toed shoes, and black pants barged into the office, unannounced and uninvited. The man spoke without identifying himself. At first he ignored Harvey. "Young lady, do you know who I am?"

Danielle was taken aback. She did not know who he was ,and she was not prepared for visitors, announced or unannounced. "No, I don't know and I don't care. Get out of my office." The words came out easily, but Danielle had no idea how she was going to back up her bluster. Harvey would be no help. In fact, at that moment, Harvey had slipped past the intruder and was attempting to exit the office.

Castro Hernandez was not accustomed to being addressed in that manner. "Lady, you need to know who I am. I am here to get the money my boss gave your father." Then looking at Harvey, "Who is this little shit?"

By now Castro was joined by another equally seedy individual. On signal from Carlos, the newcomer grabbed Harvey by the back of his shirt and literally threw him back into the office. Harvey lost his balance and crashed into a glass table between the chairs in front of the huge desk. Blood now ran freely from a gash in Harvey's forehead. Harvey looked like a small hurt child. Was he crying? It was hard to tell. If so, his tears were mixed with the blood that flowed from his wound. He was certainly whimpering, while holding a white handkerchief on his forehead.

D-Line had only one employee who knew exactly who these people were. Danielle had an idea who that might be. She would need some time to find out. She should have been terrified, but she had neither the experience nor the knowledge to be frightened. As long as her father was alive, she had no need to fear. Ignoring her sniveling little comptroller, Danielle replied forcefully. "Who are you and what are you talking about?"

"I am Castro Hernandez. I work for a man who loaned your father money." The name of Castro's employer was not forthcoming. "You owe my boss $800,000. I am here to get the money."

The desk in front of Danielle was stacked with papers, mostly bills. The light was coming on for Danielle, dimly. Her Dad was in some type of illegal business. Danielle picked up a handful of the bills. "Tell your boss that he will need to get in line."

Castro acted impatient, "Lady, my boss don't wait in no lines, and he will not take no for an answer." He then snatched Harvey from the floor. "Who are you?"

Harvey could barely stammer a reply. "Harvey Nelson. I just work here." And then volunteered, "I don't know anything."

Danielle was tired of being referred to as "Lady." "Mr. Castro, do I look like a woman with $800,000 in her pocket?"

To Castro Hernandez, she did, indeed look like a woman with $800,000. Danielle was wearing a loose fitting silk blouse, expensive looking black slacks, Jimmy Choo shoes, and he could see a Gucci alligator purse on the credenza behind the desk. Castro had noted the Mercedes SL parked outside. "It's Hernandez, lady."

Harvey looked like a stereotypical bookkeeper. Castro quickly determined that Harvey must know something about the money end of this business. Harvey was now standing, trying again to exit the office. Castro smacked Harvey with the back of his free hand and again sent him sprawling to the floor. "I will ask one more time. Who are you and what is your job?"

Harvey was now too terrified to talk at all. He was trembling, uncontrollably. Cowering, his mouth moved, but nothing came out.

Danielle moved from her place behind the desk and placed herself between Castro and Harvey. She addressed Castro. "He is just a clerk. There is no way he could know anything about any of this."

Castro then grabbed Danielle's silk blouse and backhanded her on the right side of her face, which he followed with a second slap to the left side of her face. He then looked into Danielle's eyes and appeared to flinch as he said. "Get the money together. I'll be back." With that, the two of them turned and left.

As they left, Danielle merely glared. Blood dripped from the side of her mouth, which she wiped with the back of her hand. No one had ever hit Danielle before, and she would see to it that no one ever hit her again. At that moment she did not know how, but Castro Hernandez would regret being the first and last person to ever strike Danielle Stephens.

Danielle needed information, and she could tell that it was not going to come from Harvey. She needed to talk to her father's private secretary, a woman her mother detested, and not because the secretary was sleeping with Big D. She was not. No, Danielle's mother despised Mary Alexander because Mary Alexander knew more about Big D's business than anyone else, including to her consternation, Mrs. Stephens herself. Mary Alexander knew much more than Big D would ever share with his wife. As for Danielle, all she knew was that Mary was a powerful force around the office, a person whom the employees admired and feared. Knowledge is power and Mary had both.

Danielle picked up the phone and pressed the extension for Mary's office. "Mary, come into Dad's office, I need to talk to you."

CHAPTER 5. *SAGINAW, MICHIGAN.*
Lefty Frizzell

https://www.youtube.com/watch?v=8tbrLDA18C4

Pinky and Spike, the dog, arrived at the house Ms. Saginaw owned in a middle class neighborhood which had seen better days. Susan Belinsky, her real name, got the house in her divorce. With her three children grown and out of the house, the house was larger than she needed and required more maintenance than she could afford, but the house was all she had and was near her friends, so she stayed.

Susan had truly enjoyed her trip to New Orleans until she sobered up and found herself alone, dirty, smelly, robbed, and broke, propped up outside of Harry's Corner Bar. During her remaining days in New Orleans, Susan's hatred for Pinky grew and flourished. By the time she met Jubilee Jones, she would have joyfully killed Pinky, if only she could. In this condition Susan was happy to recall the smallest detail of her time with Pinky and every detail of his interest in the man with the Range Rover.

Susan was obviously happy as she greeted Pinky, but not for the reasons Pinky assumed. Pinky got a welcoming hug and Susan's offer to go down the street for beer and pizza. Pinky was happily anticipating an evening of good food, cold beer, and satisfying sex when he heard what he thought was Susan come through the front door. It was not until he saw the agents and heard someone coming from the back of the house that his fantasies evaporated. Pinky was faced with several FBI agents in bulletproof vests carrying shotguns. It was too late for Pinky to react.

The leader of the contingent spoke. "Don't move a muscle. Don't even twitch." At about the same time, he felt the barrel of a shotgun at the back of his head. "Look straight ahead. Don't move."

Within seconds, Pinky was positioned on the floor with an agent sitting on his legs and a second kneeling on his shoulders as a third agent expertly hand cuffed his arms behind his back. For his part Spike just looked on bemused. People say dogs can have no expressions, but Spike seemed to be smiling. Pinky spoke, not to the agents, but to Spike. "What the hell are you smiling at?"

Not another word was spoken to Pinky. The agents put Pinky in the back of a car and took him downtown to a room with no windows where he sat solitarily, handcuffed, with shackles on his ankles. He yelled for water, but no one replied. The only contact with the world was a camera mounted in a corner of the room. The only furniture was the chair where he sat. This went on for hours before, without speaking, three burly agents entered the room and jerked Pinky out of the chair and drug him into a nearby bathroom pulled down his pants and sat him on a toilet. Just as soon as Pinky had finished relieving himself he was unceremoniously hauled back to the chair in the room with no windows.

Jubilee Jones had been informed of the arrest, and the local agents had been instructed that they should have no conversation with the prisoner. They did not even read Pinky his rights. To this treatment, Pinky complained often and loudly, but with no consequence. The recording device attached to the camera conveniently malfunctioned and no record would exist of the mistreatment he later claimed. Pinky was forced to sit alone and wait for whatever was to come, not even certain about why he had been arrested.

His requests, which turned to cries, for food, water, and a lawyer, if heard at all, were ignored. It was a considerably more pliable Pinky that would be brought into an office to confront his cousin, FBI Special Agent Jubilee Jones IV, nearly eight hours after the arrest.

Jubilee spoke first. "Hello, Pinky. What kind of trouble have you gotten yourself into now?"

Pinky wanted to talk to someone, anyone, and he was relieved to see his cousin. "Why are you here, cuz? I thought you worked in Memphis."

Jubilee was careful. "Pinky, I am investigating the murder of four men outside of Memphis a few weeks ago. I think you may have some information that will assist me in my investigation." A true statement, if not a totally complete statement. "You know that you have the right to remain silent and that anything you say can be used against you?" Jubilee presented Pinky with a form containing all of the magic words concerning Pinky's rights and paused while Pinky read and signed the document. The recording devices attached to the cameras in this room worked perfectly.

Pinky was relieved. He knew something about those murders, but he was not involved. Pinky's mind was spinning, *why would the FBI be involved with an investigation of murders in Tennessee?* "What makes you think I would know anything about those murders?"

Jubilee responded. "Because you worked for Daniel Stephens, and two of his employees died in that shootout."

"I didn't even know those guys. I worked at Platinum Plus. They worked for the construction company." Pinky was feeling good. Jubilee was barking up the wrong tree.

Jubilee did not miss a beat. "That's a good-looking dog you have. Is he registered?"

Pinky did not think before he answered. "I don't know. Big D gave him to me almost a year ago." Pinky was thinking, *what does that matter? Whatever, there would be no way to dispute his story; after all, Big D was not going to say otherwise.*

Jubilee continued. "What a beautiful animal. I bet he is pure bred. Have you been to New Orleans lately?"

The question got Pinky's attention. Ms. Saginaw had fingered him and had for sure told Jubilee where she and Pinky had met. "Yeah, I got trapped there during Katrina, but you already know that."

"Why were you in New Orleans in the first place?" Jubilee asked innocently.

Pinky did not like the way this line of questioning was going. He should have exercised his right to remain silent. "I just went down there to party. I should have been watching the weather reports. I got drunk with Ms. Saginaw and look what it got me."

Jubilee just wanted to keep Pinky talking. "What did it get you?"

Pinky should have shut up long ago. "This visit with you. Why are you asking me about New Orleans? I was in New Orleans a long time after the shootout in Memphis, and I don't know anything about that shootout, anyways."

Jubilee continued. "Were you with Big D in New Orleans?"

Again, Pinky should have terminated the conversation and demanded a lawyer. "No, but he must have been there. He was killed there, wasn't he?"

Jubilee persisted. "Why were you and Big D in New Orleans?"

"Who says we were together?" Pinky was confident that Ms. Saginaw had no knowledge of any relationship between Pinky and Big D. There was no way that she could.

Jubilee was going to continue asking questions until Pinky stopped talking. "Do you know Trooper Ronald Kelley?"

Now, Pinky was worried. "No, who is he?"

"Who was the man you, Big D, and Trooper Kelley went to meet in New Orleans?" Jubilee asked. "I have a video of the meeting. Would you care to see it?" With that the door opened and a female agent pushed in a metal cart on which was mounted a VCR and TV. The TV and VCR were quickly turned on for

Pinky to see. The video showed a Black Escalade from which Big D emerged. Kelley soon appeared followed by Pinky; both were kind enough to look back over their shoulder so that their faces clearly appeared on the camera. Kelley either failed to see Pinky or more likely did not know who Pinky was.

The whole episode played out for all to see. Big D and Kelley appear to speak to one another. Pinky comes up from behind and strikes Kelley with his plaster casted right arm, once in the back of the head and then in the temple area. Kelley falls striking his head violently on the pavement. Pinky drags Kelley to a wall of the Royal Sonesta Hotel and leaves the scene. Pinky is watching closely. He sees Big D approach the Lucky Dog salesman, and it appears they talk briefly. Big D then produces a large handgun and shoots the hotdog man in the chest. The hotdog man falls backwards, disappearing behind the Lucky Dog cart. Big D follows and appears to raise his gun again. Big D's head then makes an unnatural move, and he also falls to the ground. Jubilee asks that the video be stopped.

Jubilee looks at Pinky. "Who is the hotdog man and why were you meeting him?"

Pinky was finally silent, thinking… thinking that he might get something in return for the information.

Jubilee repeated the request. "Who is the hotdog man and why were Big D and Kelley meeting him?"

Pinky was stupid, or at least he did something stupid. "What's in this for me? It's not a federal crime to protect your boss from a dirty cop."

"Are you saying that Kelley is a dirty cop?" Jubilee wanted to keep Pinky talking.

Pinky did keep talking. "I'm not saying anything, unless I get something in return."

The door to the room opened and in walked an agent with the dog, Spike, and a man dressed in a white coat. Jubilee asked Pinky. "Do you know Maurice Davis?"

"Never heard of him, cuz. Why do you ask?"
Pinky had his confidence back now. He had some
information that his cousin wanted.

"Maurice Davis is one of the men you murdered
in New Orleans. You may not know his name, but you
will recall where you got this dog." Jubilee replied.

The room was cold, but Pinky now began to
sweat. "I told you, Jubilee, Big D gave me this dog over
a year ago."

Jubilee continued. "Have you ever heard of
people putting microchips in dogs so that they can be
identified if they are lost?" Jubilee knew that Pinky
would not answer. "This dog was implanted with a
microchip and the man in the white coat has read that
chip for me. Doctor, what did you learn from the
microchip implanted in this dog?"

"Well, Agent Jones, the dog is not from around
here. His name is Precious Davis. He belongs to a man
named Maurice Davis. The owner lives on Ursulines
Avenue, in New Orleans, Louisiana."

Pinky was deadly silent.

Jubilee was not finished. "Pinky you were careful not to touch anything in the home of Mr. Davis. You left no prints, nor did you leave any personal items that can be traced to you. You are a shrewd one, always have been. But you made two mistakes: the dog, and do you want to know what else?" Pinky said nothing. "You cleaned up and dried off with one of Mr. Davis's Egyptian cotton towels. Do you remember cleaning up after you killed Mr. Davis and his friend?" Sweat had visibly formed on Pinky's forehead. "We found a few hairs on that towel. Have you heard of DNA? Your DNA is on file from your last trip to prison. Guess what?" Jubilee paused for effect. "The DNA from the hairs we found on the towel in Mr. Davis's house matches yours. This is bad for you, very bad. If you will tell me why you were in New Orleans and the name of the hotdog man, I may be able to help you."

Pinky did not know that the man he had killed was the brother of a U.S. Senator. Had he known that fact, he might have also known that no one could help him, but he was now desperate. Jubilee got everything Pinky knew down to Jake's address and phone number. Pinky thought, but did not know, that the biker looking guys were the same men who had overpowered him and taken him to a deer camp. Pinky did not know who the person was who appeared to take Jake's place after the biker guys helped Jake from the scene.

Jubilee's job was done. He had been assigned the job of solving the murder of Maurice Davis, and he had accomplished that task. Many people would have washed their hands of the case. The shootout and bad drug deal were Tennessee's problems. Not Jubilee, he just had to see this thing through. The drugs and money had crossed state lines, and an associated murder had occurred in Louisiana. There had to be a federal crime in there somewhere.

CHAPTER 6. *HEART OVER MIND.*
Mel Tillis

https://www.youtube.com/watch?v=v1TCnzuJcj8

Ronald Kelley, the former head of drug enforcement for western Tennessee, could correctly be blamed for everything. It was Kelley, nearly everyone calls him by his last name, who had devised the plan in the first place. It was Kelley who had "borrowed" drugs from the evidence room with the intent of using them to rob money from a drug dealer. It was two of Kelley's partners in crime who had been killed in the shootout. It was Kelley who had been in New Orleans to reclaim the drugs and money from Jake, when plans had again gone wrong. It was Kelley who had no sooner discovered that his old nemesis Big D was the drug dealer, when he was brutally attacked by Pinky and later by two punks and left for dead as Hurricane Katrina bore down on the city.

Kelley was now medically retired from the state police and a different man, brain damaged from the vicious beating he had endured, claiming amnesia, and living with the black woman and her son who had befriended him and nursed him after the storm passed. The amnesia, the unanswered questions about the missing drugs, and especially the relationship with his girlfriend did not sit well with Kelley's father.

Kelley's father was the straight-laced chief of police in the small Arkansas town where Kelley grew up and flourished as the captain and quarterback of a legendary high school football team.

As a result of all of this history Kelley, his girlfriend Keishonda, whom Kelley called "Jackie," Keishonda's beloved son Keishon, whom Kelley called "K J," were in no man's land. Unable to live in Kelley's hometown in Arkansas (to say that Kelley's parents did not approve of the relationship would be a gross understatement) and uncomfortable in Kelley's townhouse in Memphis, K J now lived with Kelley's parents while he and Jackie commuted back and forth from Memphis.

Jackie had a solution. They would move back to her hometown, New Orleans. Jackie was going home with or without Kelley. Kelley had some money, but not enough to live comfortably in what he would consider an acceptable neighborhood in New Orleans, and Jackie had no money. What Kelley was depending on, and had not told Jackie, was money promised to him by Jake. The same money Jake and Buddy were now hiding from the FBI. The same money Big D had intended to use to buy the drugs Kelley had borrowed from the evidence room.

Kelley and Jackie were getting impatient for different reasons. Jackie was willing to move back to the 9th Ward. There was no way Kelley was going to do that. If Kelley could just get the money from Jake, they could live in a better neighborhood. That is not to say that Kelley was not acutely aware of the reality. Kelley knew well that both he and Jake were being shadowed by the FBI.

Kelley was stuck. He didn't like it, and Jackie was becoming more irritated as each day passed. Kelley was getting desperate. He needed to find a solution.

Kelley was no fool, but desperate men make irrational decisions. Kelley decided that he would again visit Jake. He would have no problem slipping the men who were watching him. Meeting with Jake, without being seen, would prove to be more difficult.

CHAPTER 7. *I'M SO LONESOME I COULD CRY.* Hank Williams

https://www.youtube.com/watch?v=4WXYjm74WFI

Danielle sat alone in her dad's office. Never had she been so sad, lonely, and anxious. Her rock, her dad, Big D, was dead, buried, and Danielle's friends had gone back to their own lives. Danielle's mother was now perpetually stoned on the drugs she had for "back pain" before Big D's demise and the new drugs prescribed for the stress associated with Big D's death. Danielle's husband, that worthless sack of shit, was spending all of his time "managing" Platinum Plus. He seldom came home at all. On top of everything else, the FBI had raided the office of D-Line Construction, and had taken the books. Not to mention, her comptroller, Harvey, was in the mental hospital suffering from a nervous breakdown.

As Danielle sat brooding, she came to the conclusion that she had few choices. She had considered bankruptcy, but she was fairly certain that her dad would have hidden money for emergencies.

Danielle had consulted a bankruptcy lawyer and had been advised that to fail to disclose assets in bankruptcy was a crime. Further, unlike the crimes she now realized her father had probably committed, to now fail to disclose assets in the bankruptcy would be on her. Moreover, bankruptcy would have no effect on Castro Hernandez and his boss, whoever that was. It was all on her. The party that had been her life up to this point was over.

Big D was an optimist and a survivor. She knew that her father had been in financial troubles before and that he had found a way out. Perhaps, she thought, an illegal way out, but a way out. Danielle determined that she could, too. Now all she needed to do was to quit whining and figure out how. She was not going to live in poverty. Danielle was an optimist, too. No matter how bad it looks, there is always some good news somewhere. Danielle just needed to start looking.

Earlier meetings with Mary Alexander had been as unhelpful as had her meeting with Harvey. Danielle was convinced that Mary could help her, but Mary did not trust Danielle and she was unwilling to share the information Danielle needed.

Danielle was perceptive and determined. She had searched her family home, just ahead of the FBI. Her search revealed a secret compartment. The secret compartment contained over $100,000 in cash and two items which would prove to be particularly valuable. Danielle now had a tool that was certain to loosen Mary's tongue.

Danielle again summoned Mary to her dad's office. Mary reluctantly entered the office and walked the twenty feet from the door to one of the opulent red leather chairs placed carefully in front of the desk. Mary sat down impatiently. "What do you want now, Danielle?"

Danielle wasted no time "I found this little book at Dad's house. I know you have seen this book before?" And Danielle thought, *I bet you have been looking for it.*

Mary replied uncomfortably. "Yes. I've have seen that book." She did not add, *I have been looking for that book.*

The book contained a list of cash payments to Mary Alexander and her initials showing receipt of the payments. Big D expected loyalty and when possible he hedged his bets and insured loyalty. If Mary had found the book first, she would have been long gone.

Danielle switched on the big screen TV mounted over the fireplace and turned up the sound. She then walked around the desk and quietly asked Mary. "Do you think that the FBI has bugged this office?"

Mary was impressed, her father's daughter. Mary also saw that it was time to cooperate. "No, I had our IT man check on that. Your dad has equipment installed which will detect any surveillance from anyone. He was careful about such things. No one, except for the IT man, your dad, and me know about the devices. I doubt that the FBI even knows. "

Danielle retreated to her Dad's chair and turned off the TV. I have a number of questions for you and I better get straight answers. "Where was all of the cash coming from? Where did he get the money to pay you? How did the company get by without paying suppliers and sub-contractors?"

Mary paused before she answered. She was trapped, but she was not the type to give up easily. "You need to ask Harvey. He is the comptroller."

"Don't bullshit me, Mary. You know Harvey is a helpless little wimp. He's not going to admit that he knows anything. Just hit the high points, and I'll fill in the details."

Mary had never paid taxes on the money Big D had paid her and if this book landed in the hands of the FBI, tax evasion would be the least of her problems. The book would tie her to drug dealing and perhaps the deaths in Brownsville. Maybe by helping Danielle, Mary could save herself.

Mary responded with a threat. "You must understand one thing and you must never forget this one thing: I know all of the details and I know everything the FBI wants. I can even incriminate you."

Perhaps a vacant threat, Danielle had done nothing wrong. How, thought Danielle, up until a few days ago she had only been in this building to get money from her father. *What if my dad hid money in my name?* "Did my dad have money hidden

somewhere? Is some of that money in my name?"
Danielle failed to mention the $100,000 she had found
in the wall of her dad's house.

Mary thought to herself as she responded; *her
father's daughter indeed,* "I'll help you, but remember,
if I go down, you go down."

Danielle wasn't worried about "going down."
What she wanted was to protect the image of her father.
Danielle was content to let Mary think she had
intimidated her. Mary could think whatever she wanted
to think as long as Danielle got some answers.

Mary hesitated, but the more she thought about
it, the more she wanted to tell Danielle, everything. As
she began to talk, it was cathartic. Before long facts
were spilling from Mary like dirt from a dump truck.
Danielle and Mary spent the rest of the day together,
into the night. By evening they were partners. They
both had loved Big D. They both wanted to protect his
image. They were partners, but more like sisters. They
were united in their determination to save the company
and in the process, themselves.

Mary's initial revelations were hardly news at all to Danielle. Danielle had done her homework, and she knew everything that could be determined from the legitimate books of the company and the little book that had loosened Mary's tongue. Nonetheless, she listened intently, more to see if Mary was accurate and truthful than to learn anything.

Mary told Danielle that D-Line Construction had three ongoing projects: an office building in Nashville, a medical clinic in Jackson, and an addition to a church in Memphis. Each project was managed by a competent superintendent, and each project was underbid. Danielle was not surprised to learn that money skimmed from Platinum Plus was being laundered through the projects, but she was shocked to learn that drug money was also being laundered through the projects. She was likewise not surprised to learn that her worthless husband was now wasting the profits from Platinum Plus on girls, booze, and cocaine.

Mary was amazed by how unemotional Danielle remained as the sad facts were revealed. Danielle took it all in, scheming all the while. When Mary appeared to be finished, Danielle asked, "Who is

Castro Hernandez and why does he claim I owe him $800,000?"

Mary knew those details, too. "You heard about the shootout in Brownsville?" Danielle nodded. "Your dad and a partner, Castro's boss, had arranged to buy heroin from a drug dealer. The deal was too big for your dad alone. The drugs were already sold. You could liken your dad to a wholesaler; he only dealt in large quantities, and he always had them sold before he bought them. The source in the Brownsville deal was a fairly new one, but prior deals with this same supplier had gone off without a problem. According to Jessie (an employee of D-Line who had survived the shootout), something went wrong and everybody started shooting. Two of your dad's employees and two others were killed. The two "others" turned out to be undercover narcs."

Danielle was intrigued. The money and the drugs could be her salvation, if she could get them. "Where are the drugs and the money now?"

"A stockbroker from Shreveport somehow ended up with the drugs and the money. Your father sent two men to Shreveport to retrieve the money and the drugs, but only one returned, empty handed. Your father was in New Orleans to meet with the stockbroker when he was killed. As far as I know, the stockbroker still has the drugs and the money."

"Is there any other hidden money?' Danielle asked as she produced the other items she had recovered from the wall of her dad's house. The items were two identical flat keys with numbers stamped on them. "What do these keys fit? A safety deposit box?"

Mary had wondered where those keys were hidden. Not that knowing it would have done her any good. "Yes, a safety deposit box in your father's name. No one else was allowed in the box." Mary had warned Big D that he should allow someone else, her, access to the box, but he had refused. "There is no way you will ever get to that money. If you could, it would help. I bet there are several hundred thousand dollars in that box. Probably cash and almost certainly some gold coins." Mary had seen the gold coins, and they were now missing. She presumed that they would be in the box.

"Where is the safety deposit box? I assume it is not at our regular bank."

Mary was again impressed. "No, it's in a small bank out in Germantown.''

Danielle was using her extraordinary mind, for the first time. Mary interrupted Danielle's thoughts. "A lot of good those keys will do you. I bet the FBI is checking every bank in Tennessee and Arkansas for bank accounts and bank boxes in your dad's name. You could get in with a court order, or you can wait and let the FBI tell you what's in that box. Either way you will get nothing."

As Mary left the room, she heard Danielle say under her breath. "There must be a way. There's always a way."

CHAPTER 8. *SHE THINKS I STILL CARE.*
George Jones

https://www.youtube.com/watch?v=96hwaRPMVe8

Jake had to knock on the door to his own house. The locks had been changed after Jen threw him out. Jen's sister and brother had returned to south Louisiana, but Jake did not know exactly where. Jen's father was in Chalmette helping to place a FEMA trailer in the front yard of the family home. Jen's father and mother would be forced to live in that trailer until their house could be rebuilt. It would be necessary to first gut the house and remove all sheetrock so that the mold could be removed.

As luck would have it, Jen's mother answered the door. She just looked at him with undisguised hatred, turned, and walked away. Jake stood alone in the doorway, suitcase in hand, not knowing if he still wanted to come home. Pondering and immobile, Jake stood until his daughter came into sight at the top of the stairs. More beautiful than her mother and glowing with life, pregnant, or so Jen said, she stood looking at her father.

At first, neither spoke. To his discredit Jake had not thought about what he would say to his only daughter. Eloise spoke first. "Hi, Dad. I heard you might be coming home."

The ice was broken. Jake replied. "Eloise you look great. I am so glad to see you." Eloise made her way down the stairs. Jake hoped that she would come close, and when she did, he hugged her affectionately.

Eloise returned the hug. "I'm happy that you're home." Concerning Jake's homecoming the score was one against and one for; Jen would cast the deciding vote.

Jake tentatively entered his own house. He could hear noises emanating from the kitchen. As he entered the room, Jen was bent over unloading clean dishes from the dishwasher. Jen's outstanding rear end was on display. Jake was ready, he announced. "I'm home."

Jen stood up and turned to her husband. "Thanks." They hugged. The hug was neither here nor there, neither acceptance nor rejection. The score was still tied.

Jake wondered. *Will this work? Can I make this work again? Do I want to make this work?* As they embraced, he became certain of only one thing. He did want to make it work.

Jake had to know. "What did you tell Jubilee Jones?"

The question was one Jen expected, but not so soon. "Aren't you going to ask how I feel? Don't you want to know how your daughter is coping?"

Jake was thinking of himself first. Not such a good start. "Of course, I do. You both look fine. Eloise looks better, if that is possible. How do you feel?"

"Physically I feel fine. Emotionally I'm a wreck. It's time for you to bow up and assume your responsibilities."

Jake wondered. *Why is everything always my fault? She comes into my room naked, what did she expect me to do? Think about birth control? And Eloise, she is over 20 years old, don't they teach sex ed at S.M.U.?* Jake kept his thought to himself. "I have thought of little except for you and Eloise for two days.

I am here now and I am here to stay, if you will let me. We will get through this. We have done it before and we can do it again." Jake had thought of one other thing. He had thought a lot about one other thing: what had Jen told Jubilee Jones? He knew better than to ask again, so he changed the subject. "Where should I put my suitcase?"

Jen's response was no great surprise. "Let's take it slow, Jake. How about the guest bedroom for now?"

What could he say? Under his breath he mumbled, "I suppose a welcome-home blow job would be totally out of the question."

Jake spoke just a little too loud, and Jen's hearing was better than most. Jen heard him and snapped, "What did you say?"

"All I said was, okay." He did not add, *how long is "for now"*? Jake had resolved that he would stay in the guest room only as long as his mother-in-law remained in the house. He wanted his life back; he really did, but not at any cost. Jake was not going to live the rest of his life in a one-way marriage. Maybe the better question was, *could Jen ever truly forgive him?*

Jen ignored Jake's smart aleck remark. "I plan to make this work."

They were both thinking the same thing: *for the sake of the unborn babies.* Neither voiced the thought.

As Jake headed to the guest bedroom, Jen spoke. She knew what Jake was thinking. "I never told Jubilee a thing. After he called, I called Tim. Tim told me that I should not under any circumstances tell Jubilee anything. His exact words were 'nobody talks, everybody walks.' He told me that I was to tell Jubilee that he would need to call Tim if he wanted to know anything. You better take the same advice."

Jake almost screamed: *thank God and Hallelujah,* but instead he asked, "Did you tell Tim about the 'problem'?"

"No, he told me that he would talk to you when you got home. Tim said that the FBI might concoct some theory to override the attorney-client privilege by claiming that I was not the client especially if we got divorced. He did ask if a woman was involved, you and 'some woman.' "

Jake was hungry for information. "What did you tell him?"

Jen was always smarter than Jake. "I just rolled my eyes. Let him believe what he wants to believe. This town is too small. I think we should take Tim's advice and talk to no one, including Tim."

Jake had to agree. "You're right. I'm keeping my mouth shut."

CHAPTER 9. *IN THE JAILHOUSE NOW.*
Webb Pierce

https://www.youtube.com/watch?v=kiVDtll8th0

Pinky was back in Memphis and cooperating with Jubilee to the utmost. He even suggested that he take Jubilee to the well in Louisiana where he would find the remains of Mario Prince (the man Jake had killed) and Jake's dog. The dog who had attacked Pinky and been killed by him in the struggle.

Pinky was eager to help for selfish reasons. Most of all, he wanted to avoid the needle, and he also saw the trip as an opportunity to escape solitary confinement, if only for a while. Pinky was thrilled when Jubilee agreed that he could accompany two agents from Memphis to the site. There was another unstated reason Pinky wanted to go. Pinky saw the trip as an opportunity for him to escape. He did not know how, but if he was ever to escape it would not be from his prison cell. Pinky enthusiastically accompanied the two well-trained, if somewhat green, agents on the road trip from Memphis to Shreveport.

The six-hour trip to Shreveport was uneventful. Pinky sat in the back, handcuffed and shackled. There were no handles on the inside of the back doors and a steel screen separated him from the two agents. The means for Pinky to escape was not revealing itself. At least Pinky was being treated to a view of Arkansas and Louisiana as opposed to the view of the walls of his jail cell. Pinky spent the night in a jail cell in Shreveport. The trio made their way to Mansfield early the next morning.

The well Pinky had been shown was located in a deer camp leased by the Ebarb brothers and others in Desoto Parish, north and west of Mansfield, not too far from Longstreet. The well where Jake deposited Mario Prince and his dog was located at a deer camp on land owned by Jake's family in Bossier Parish north and east of Benton. The two wells were 70 miles apart. Further, when Buddy learned that the FBI was looking into Jake's problem, Buddy had a friend with an oil field vacuum truck clean out the well containing the remains and then arranged for the contents of the well to be pumped into a salt water disposal well. After the well was cleaned out, Buddy borrowed a backhoe, destroyed

and filled in the well, and then arranged for the timber
in the field to be clear cut. It would be virtually
impossible for anyone to now locate the remains of
Mario Prince. Pinky was going to show the FBI the
wrong well and lose the little credibility he had.

Desoto Parish deputies met the FBI agents and
Pinky at the Sheriff's office in Mansfield. The deputies
knew the Ebarb brothers and knew exactly where the
camp in question was located. The FBI agents were
left to wonder why the deputies were so concerned
about whether there could be any confrontation with the
Ebarb brothers or other members of the deer club with
rights to hunt on the lease. The deputies seemed to be
relieved to learn that a search warrant had been issued
from a federal court and had been served on one of the
Ebarb brothers, who had expressed some curiosity, but
no objection. Nevertheless, the deputies insisted that
four ridiculously well-armed deputies in two cars
accompany the FBI agents and the FBI forensic team to
the well.

Samples were gathered, without incident, from
the well. The initial test result revealed no human
remains, no canine remains. The final results would not

be available for days, but the forensic team was convinced at the site that they had been misled.

When the preliminary results were provided to Jubilee, he was surprised. Jubilee knew Pinky and had been convinced by his story. Jubilee remained convinced that there was truth to his story. After hearing Pinky's story, Jubilee had searched for the missing Mario Prince without success. Mario had not reported to his parole officer, and the last time anyone had seen him he had been with Pinky. Jubilee pondered these facts and decided that it was time for him to visit Shreveport and the enigmatic stockbroker, James Cane.

By the time the agents and Pinky left the well, it was well past lunch time. The agents chose to take Highway 171 back to Shreveport. On the way they stopped at a gas station, convenience store, café combination for a late lunch. Pinky was allowed to exit the car to have his lunch at the makeshift dining area located in the establishment. All three men were enjoying a good Louisiana bar-b-que sandwich when two wild eyed, masked black men entered the store, produced automatic weapons and ordered everyone onto the floor.

The two almost immediately recognized that Pinky was a prisoner and that the men with him were some kind of cops. One of the men went to empty the cash register while the other kept his weapon trained on the FBI agents. "Remove your guns, both of you. Be real careful, this gun has a hair trigger." The officers did as they were told; to do otherwise would have risked the lives of several civilians and employees. "Take those handcuffs off of the prisoner." The officer did as he was told.

"You, yeah you." Now directing his instructions to Pinky, "Handcuff those two together." Pinky gladly complied.

Pinky picked up one of the guns. "You, give me the keys to your truck." The demand was directed at the most prosperous looking of the clientele. Every vehicle in the parking lot, save the FBI car, was a pickup truck. "Which truck is yours? Come with me and show me. If you pick the wrong truck, I will shoot you and get someone else's truck." Now free and holding an FBI issued Glock, Pinky was immensely more intimidating than were the two robbers.

The robbers left after first shooting out the tires of the FBI car. Pinky left in the opposite direction in the stolen truck, a late model Ford F-150, a truck he would need to ditch as soon as possible.

CHAPTER 10. *CRYSTAL CHANDELIER.*
Carl Belew

https://www.youtube.com/watch?v=Jo_E-MLhq7I

Danielle sat in the office of the vice-president of a small bank in Germantown, Tennessee. The young VP was less than ten years older than Danielle. The young girl had no idea that Danielle was Big D's daughter. In fact, the girl did not even know who Big D was, nor did she know that Big D had a safety deposit box at that same bank. She was preoccupied with her own upcoming wedding. The girl showed off her engagement ring with great pride. Under other circumstances Danielle might have scoffed, but today she admired the ring and listened carefully to the girl's plans. "We are getting married on Saturday night. The reception will be at TPC Southwind. We have been planning for months. I am excited and at the same time ready for the whole thing to be over. Are you married? Do you want to have your husband on the account?"

Danielle had not worn her wedding ring and had intentionally dressed down. No fancy shoes, no Gucci purse. "No, I am not married. It will just be me on the account. Are you going on a trip for your honeymoon?"

The news that Danielle, pretty but overweight, was not married dampened the mood. The VP thought that she best get back to work. "Yes I will be out all of next week, but don't worry: if you need to get into the box one of the tellers will help you."

When Danielle returned to the office, she learned from Mary that Castro Hernandez and a companion were there to see her. Castro's companion was the same man who had attacked poor Harvey. Once again, they had arrived unannounced and had barged into Big D's office. This time Danielle was ready. Unbeknownst to nearly everyone, especially Castro and his companion, Big D's office was a fortress, built by Big D. The room had impenetrable locks on its only door and steel shutters which could be controlled remotely. (And from the office, but Danielle now disabled that feature when she was out of the office). Mary and Danielle Sat in Mary's office with the controls to Big D's office. As Castro waited he saw the shutters closing and heard the clang of the door locking. Simultaneously, the big screen TV over the fireplace sprang into life.

Castro had his gun drawn as he attempted in vain to open the door. Had the room not been sound proofed the reports from his gun would have undoubtedly been heard as he tried to blast his way out of the room. Danielle's face appeared on the TV screen. "You are wasting you ammo and your time. You will not leave this room until and unless I let you. I told you that I had no money. Why are you back?"

Castro's first impulse was to shoot out the TV and he was about to do just that when his cohort stopped him. "Castro, vamos a escuchar lo que la mujer tiene que decir." With that, Danielle muted the microphone and turned to Mary. "He said roughly, let's hear what the woman has to say."

Again Mary was impressed. "Do you speak Spanish?"

"A little, un poco." Danielle replied as she turned her mic back on.

Castro then saw the camera, actually one of several cameras. "Look bitch. You better open the door, now."

Danielle just looked on bemused. "Who is your boss?"

Castro would have rather died than to disclose the name of his boss. "That's not your concern. What you need to know is that he wants his money and that I will not leave here until you give me the money."

Before he finished his reply, a small door, more of a peephole, opened behind Big D's desk. Simultaneously the barrel of a rifle appeared from the peephole and fired one shot grazing Castro's left ear. The barrel moved ever so slightly so that it was now trained on Castro's chest. Danielle spoke again. "I don't have any money. My dad is dead, and if i don't get some answers, it is likely that you will die very soon. Tell me the name and whereabouts of your boss. I want to deal directly with him and only with him."

"I am not going to tell you anything. Now open this door before I shoot up your entire office." With that statement completed, a second round left the gun in the peephole, the bullet hit Castro squarely in the center of his chest. Within seconds Castro lay dead on the office floor.

Danielle showed no emotion, muted the mic and said to Mary. "That's one son-of-a-bitch who won't be hitting me again."

Now only one live person remained imprisoned in the office. The man was, predictably, terrified. "Quien es tu jefe?" Danielle inquired a third time. This time in Spanish.

The man could hardly speak for two reasons, terror and the fact that English was not his first, and by no means his best, language. He answered in Spanish. "Castro es mi jefe. El Gran jefe no se quien es."

Mary sat in her office with Danielle. Danielle interpreted. "He says that Castro was his boss. He does not know the name of the big boss." Mary motioned for Danielle to turn off the camera and microphone. After the microphone and camera were off, Mary spoke. "I think you should have shot this one first... I think he is telling the truth."

Danielle did not hesitate. She spoke to the man holding the gun through the peephole "Shoot the son-of-a-bitch, get them out of my office and get the office cleaned up."

Danielle turned to Mary. "When these punks turn up missing, I bet we will hear from the 'Boss.'"

Mary just looked on in awe. *Big D's daughter, for sure.*

The next Friday morning Danielle appeared at the bank and signed in for a visit to her safety deposit box. Behind her, Danielle dragged a large rolling brief case. The young VP Danielle had dealt with the week before was undoubtedly enjoying her honeymoon on some tropical island. Danielle approached a teller, one that looked young and inexperienced, and asked to be let into her safety box. In her pocket Danielle had two sets of keys. Danielle signed the sheet for her box. It was the first time she had been in the box since she opened it the week before. The young girl secured the master key for all of the safety deposit boxes and led Danielle into the vault.

Danielle waited for the teller to speak. "What is your box number? Give me your key, please."

Danielle produced a key and handed it to the teller. "It is box 101. See it down there."

The teller used the key Danielle gave her and the master key. The teller easily opened safety deposit box 101. The teller was totally unaware of the fact that the safety deposit box she opened did not belong to Danielle Gentry. No, the box did not belong to

Danielle Gentry. Box 101, the box the teller opened belonged to Daniel Stephens. The teller left Danielle alone in the vault. Danielle kept the key to her own safety box in her pocket. The plan had worked to perfection. In a matter of minutes Danielle had put on cotton gloves and had emptied her dad's box. She left the bank with a rolling brief case containing 70 Krugerrands and over $200,000 in cash.

There are no cameras in vaults containing safety deposit boxes. No one would ever know. That is not to say that the FBI never found the box. They did find it, they did obtain a subpoena, and they did drill open the box. They found nothing, not even finger prints. Only cotton filaments from the gloves Danielle had immediately disposed of after leaving the bank.

Danielle was in charge. She was determined to keep D-Line Construction afloat. She now had a buffer. She just needed a plan.

CHAPTER 11. *I'M TIRED.* Webb Pierce

https://www.youtube.com/watch?v=SAzYlqrbL38

Jake had never been much of a drinker, but his habits were changing and not for the better. Living with three women would have been bad enough even if one of them didn't detest him and the other two weren't pregnant. Jake was miserable, and he spent most nights in the back den drinking and flipping TV channels.

Buddy had a girlfriend, as he periodically did, and Jake was not seeing him as much as usual. Buddy's affair would not last; Jake knew that and Buddy knew that, too. Buddy was not going to commit to any woman. The affair, like all of the others before, was doomed.

Buddy called Jake early on a rainy Saturday morning. "You want to get some breakfast?"

Jake would have accepted an invitation to a gay ball, just to get out of the house. "Sure, let me get cleaned up. I'll meet you at Strawn's in 45 minutes."

Buddy was already seated at a table drinking coffee and talking to a young man wearing khaki pants, nondescript shoes, and a beige shirt. The man left to join a group of similarly attired men at a big round table in the back of the restaurant.

"Good morning, Buddy. Who is the guy with the shit-eating grin you were talking to?"

"Jake that's not a shit-eating grin, that's a religious glow. He is one of the assistants at the Baptist Church on Youree Drive. Wants me to join his Bible study back there."

Jake knew how Buddy felt about organized religion. "I take it you declined?"

"No Jake, I offered to conduct the class myself. I told him the class would be short. 'Do unto others as you would have them do unto you.' End of class, and we can all go to the Cub (a nearby bar) and get a Bloody Mary. He didn't embrace my suggestion."

Jake refused to let it go. This was fun. "Why not, doesn't he think you know the Bible?"

Buddy was ready to move on. "Probably because it is unnatural for a man to treat another man as he would himself. Man is by nature selfish and greedy. You of all people should know that. People aren't investing money with you for the good of mankind as a whole."

Jake was thinking about what Buddy had said and working on a clever response, when a pleasant looking, average-sized black man in cheap gray slacks and a short sleeve white shirt walked up and said, "Good morning, Mr. Hawkins and Mr. Cane, my name is Jubilee Jones. Please call me Jubilee. May I sit down?"

Somehow, Jake had never gotten around to calling Jubilee back. They should have said no and left the restaurant, but Jubilee was so polite and appeared so harmless that Buddy said, "Sure, have a seat. Can I buy you a cup of coffee?"

Jubilee sat down and began to speak. "You two look enough alike to be brothers, even twins."

Jake responded. "That's what people say. Buddy's actually older, but better preserved."

Jubilee continued. "Yes, Mathew does look good. Did you know that Buddy's real name is Mathew?"

Jake did know, few did, but said nothing, remembering Jen's advice.

"Mathew was quite a soldier. Did you know that, James?"

Jake knew that Buddy had been in the Army, knew that Buddy had been hurt, but that was all he knew. Jake nodded in a way that revealed nothing.

"Yes, Mathew was not only a Distinguished Expert Marksman, but his scores have never been beaten. There are several medals that you have never accepted, Mathew. Why didn't you take your medals?"

Buddy did not respond.

"Mathew..."

Buddy interrupted, "Please call me Buddy, everyone calls me Buddy."

"Buddy, tell me how you were able to commandeer that helicopter and fly it out to the aircraft carrier? Especially with your shot up leg. You were a Green Beret, an infantry soldier; you had never flown a helicopter. You saved a bunch of good soldiers with that deed. How did you do it?"

Jake had never heard any of this. Marksman? Green Beret? Helicopter? Jake had known Buddy for almost 20 years, and Buddy and not once spoken a word of any of this.

Buddy spoke. "I had flown many missions in helicopters. I watched the pilots. It's not rocket science. You'd be surprised by what you can do when you have no other choice."

Buddy never acknowledged the questions about the medals or the combat, but he seemed somewhat proud of flying that helicopter.

"Enough about me, what can we do for you Mr. Jones?"

"Call me Jubilee. Actually, there are a lot of things you can clear up for me. I'm not sure exactly where I should start."

Buddy did not wait for any questions from Jubilee. "Captain Jones, it was? You are also an Army man and a man I would have been proud to have as my superior. I like you, I kinda knew I would. If not for the fact that you are here as a Special Agent of the FBI, we would love to talk with you about many things. But, as you well know, one must be very careful when talking to an FBI agent. Many people have served time in jail for what they said to an FBI agent. Many of those people were never convicted of the crime being investigated by the agent. Jubilee, no offense, we are going to exercise our right to remain silent."

Jubilee was undeterred. "You fellows have been model citizens, Buddy, in service to his country, and you, Jake. Can I call you Jake? In service to your community and family."

Jake and Buddy remained silent.

"How did you two get tied up with the likes of Daniel Stephens, Sidney Jones, and Ronald Kelley? How did you get their drugs and dirty money? What have you done with the drugs and the money? These are things I need to know. I will get my answers. I always get my answers."

Jake was noticeably squirming. *How does he know so much?* Buddy showed no emotion, he was thinking. *I bet they are searching our houses at this very moment.*

Jubilee stood up to leave. "Enjoy your breakfast. I must leave now. I need to supervise the execution of five search warrants. One each, for your house and shop, Buddy, and the others for your house, your rent house, and your office, Jake. When I am done, I want both of you to come to the local office for further questioning."

After Jubilee left, Buddy ate a hardy breakfast. Jake had trouble keeping down his coffee.

"Buddy, why aren't they searching the camp and my cart barn at Palmetto (the golf club where Jake played)?"

"Oh, they will. Just give them time to find out they exist. And by the way, they searched Ebarb's camp yesterday with Pinky's help. They found nothing. Good thing we took Pinky to Ebarb's camp. But, that's not the big news."

Jake's was about to lose his coffee. "What is the big news?" He asked not really wanting to know.

"Pinky escaped."

There would soon be more big news about Pinky, very soon.

CHAPTER 12. *THAT'S ALL RIGHT.*
Elvis Preseley

https://www.youtube.com/watch?v=2fXCrYEPKjs

Kelley continued to claim amnesia with regard to anything associated with the shootout or the missing drugs. Kelley's superiors and the FBI often made trips to Arkansas to talk to him. Kelley was spending most of his time with Jackie, in Memphis, but when the authorities called, he inevitably retreated to his parent's house in Arkansas.

Kelley never offered any information, but in the process his father, Chief Kelley, learned plenty. The man was no fool, and he had put two and two together. Chief Kelley knew that his son knew more than he was saying, but what bothered him more was his son's relationship with Jackie.

It was not that he disliked Jackie. He actually liked her and, in spite of himself, he loved her son KJ. He sometimes found himself forgetting that KJ was black. On the other hand, he never forgot that Jackie was black. He had to blame his son's relationship with a "nigger" on someone.

Chief Kelley listened carefully for what the state police and the FBI had discovered. Through his considerable skills, connections, and experience, he was able to learn that a man by the name of Sidney Jones, AKA Pinky, had been the one who had assaulted his son and, in the process, Chief Kelly reasoned, somehow turned his son into a "nigger lover." It made him sick and ashamed. He had to do something. He resolved, for starters, that he would track down this Pinky fellow and punish him for what he had done to his son.

Chief Kelley was disappointed when he learned that the FBI had arrested Pinky. He had to find a way to get to Pinky. In Chief Kelley's mind, jail was too good for Pinky. He kept in touch, eager for an opening. His opening came when he learned that the FBI was taking Pinky to Louisiana to look for a dead body.

Chief Kelley put on civilian clothes. In his case, the only civilian clothes he owned was a combination church and funeral suit. He then gathered his .38 Smith & Wesson Special service revolver and his shotgun, a Remington 870 with an eighteen and one half-inch barrel. He holstered the .38 and put the shotgun in the passenger seat of his wife's Buick and headed to Mansfield, Louisiana.

Chief Kelley had a former employee who now worked for the Desoto Parish Sherriff, so he concocted a story about a fellow in Mansfield he needed to question and arranged to meet his former employee on the same day that the FBI agents and Pinky were scheduled to arrive. The deputy he met was surprised to see Chief Kelley out of uniform. The FBI agents and Pinky were in the office at the same time, but neither these agents nor Pinky knew Kelley, and they had no reason to be the least bit suspicious of his presence.

Chief Kelley addressed the Desoto Paris deputy. "I am just checking in out of courtesy. The man I want to talk to is not dangerous. I don't need any backup. You seem busy here. I'll call if I need anything." The deputy was indeed busy, busy worrying about the Ebarbs, and he was more than happy to send Chief Kelley out with no escort.

Kelley left the sheriff's office first and waited patiently for the entourage assembled for the search to pass. He soon learned that shadowing people who have no reason to suspect that they might be followed in a nondescript Buick is easy, especially for a man of Chief Kelley's experience. He had no reason to trail the group into the woods. There were entirely too many people in the group. He knew this, but what he did not know was just how he was going to get to Pinky. Chief Kelley just had a feeling that he would.

His break was delivered many hours later as he sat a half a mile from a gas station, convenience store, café combination- waiting. It was then that Kelly saw two out-of-place black punks enter the store while pulling on masks. He knew exactly what was happening and, under other circumstances, would have jumped at the chance to assist. Instead he found himself smiling at the fact that the unsuspecting crooks would soon be confronted by two highly trained FBI agents and either end up dead or in custody. In the confusion, maybe, just maybe, he would end up with sole custody of Pinky.

Chief Kelley was stunned a few minutes later when the two crooks emerged from the store carrying what looked like the contents of the cash register, and he was even more shocked to see Pinky following them.

Kelley's car was running before Pinky arrived at the Ford truck he would use for his getaway. As Pinky sped off, he found himself behind a nondescript Buick that had passed by just as he left the parking lot of the store.

The first road Chief Kelley came to was La. 172. He turned left towards Keachi. Pinky followed, just as the Chief had predicted. Pinky was getting off of the main road as fast as he could. Chief Kelley drove ahead slightly in excess of the speed limit, casually glancing at Pinky in his rear view mirror as he drove. They drove on in tandem for several miles. Several times it seemed that Pinky was about to pass. They were in a rural area, but there were houses on both sides of the road. Suddenly, Pinky turned off of the highway and up the driveway of a house with an open garage as well as a somewhat larger barn or shop. Kelley drove on until he was out of sight and then turned around.

When Kelley returned there was no sign of the Ford truck or of Pinky. He did notice a Honda Accord in an open garage, more like a three sided carport with no door, near the house. Kelley turned into the next door neighbor's driveway a quarter of a mile away shielded from view by a hedge and some trees. Kelley parked the Buick in the driveway of the adjacent property. Through the trees he could now see the Ford truck hidden behind the shop next door. After he exited his car and made his way to the hedge he could also see the back door of the house that had been kicked in and was open, swinging in the breeze.

Kelley had no time to waste. There was a gate and a path through the hedge between the two houses. Kelley made his way through the gate and into a garage where a Honda Accord sat. He stationed himself in front of the Honda with his shotgun in hand, a shell in the chamber. Chief Kelley crouched down in front of the car and waited. He didn't have to wait long. Within a few minutes, he heard footsteps coming from the house toward the garage. Through a dirty window Kelley caught a glimpse. It was Pinky all right, the difference was that he was now out of the orange jumpsuit and dressed in ill-fitting jeans, a baseball cap and an LSU sweatshirt. He carried what appeared to be car keys in his right hand. The gun was out of sight, probably tucked into his belt. Kelley was right. *He is*

*coming for the Honda. He needs to get out of the
pickup truck as fast as he can.*

All Kelley knew was police work. It was all he
had done his entire life. Some might say that he was
lucky to have to have predicted Pinky's every move,
but it was not luck. Pinky tried the door to the Honda.
It was locked. He bent over to put the key in the lock
when he saw out of the side of his eye an old man stand
up in front of the car. Pinky reached under the
sweatshirt for his gun, but before he could grab it the
first blast from the shotgun hit him somewhere between
his stomach and his chest. The second blast caught the
side of his head, as the force of the first blast knocked
him backwards and sideways.

Kelley looked down at Pinky's mangled body.
He had expected that he would feel relief if not joy.
Instead, he felt nothing. *Should he call the Sherriff?*
Kelly looked at Pinky again. Nothing, no relief, no joy,
no feeling of satisfaction, nothing. Chief Kelley
surveyed the scene. He had not touched a thing. There
were no footprints on the concrete floor of the garage.
He stepped over the body and retraced his steps to his
car parked next door. No footprints on the path. No

one was anywhere around. He looked for surveillance cameras, none anywhere.

Kelly analyzed the situation. Why go through the trouble of telling the sheriff. All that will bring is a lot of unnecessary paperwork and a bunch of questions from the sheriff and the FBI. Some of those questions might be hard to answer. Kelley slid into the driver's seat of the Buick, calmly backed up, and slowly drove east on La. 172. Before long he had reached La. 175, and then I-49.

Chief Kelley had avenged the sins of his son. Why did he feel nothing? He would have many hours during the drive home to contemplate this question. If Chief Kelley had thought about it, he might have realized that there was another missing feeling -- guilt. He did not have that feeling either. By midnight he was home.

The owners of the house, barn, and Honda were off on a trip in their motorhome. It would be the next day before a search party organized for that purpose would find the remains of Sidney "Pinky" Jones. The stolen Glock pistol was still in the waistband of his stolen jeans. Jubilee was unable to talk his superiors into allowing him to investigate the death of his cousin. The person or persons responsible for the death were never identified.

CHAPTER 13. *COLD COLD HEART.*
Hank Williams

https://www.youtube.com/watch?v=Wn2e4Dhod7M

Danielle's husband, the well-connected Danny Gentry, came home early on a Sunday morning to find his belongings piled in the driveway. Billy Mac McClendon, an iron worker, turned foreman, and most recently, enforcer for Big D, sat waiting in a company truck.

Billy Mac was not yet 30, but he had seen and lived a lot. His entire family were iron workers, and he started while still in school. Before he was 25, he had worked in 15 states and had been arrested, mostly for fighting, in nine. A powerful man and an accomplished fighter, Billy Mac seldom had fights that lasted past his first punch. Several times he would have likely stayed in jail but for the fact that he was also an excellent worker, loyal, skilled, and dependable. These qualities caused his superiors to do whatever was necessary to get him out of jail and back on the job. It was all of these talents that caught the attention of Big D, who put Billy Mac on the payroll as a foreman.

Danny was drunk and high on cocaine. He knew Billy Mac. "Billy Mac, what the fuck is going on? What are you doing here?"

Billy Mac was not much of a talker. "I work for Ms. Stephens now. Give me the keys to your Porsche, the keys to Platinum Plus, load your shit in this pickup and get your ass out of here."

"She's my wife. Her name is Mrs. Gentry; now get out of my way."

"Danny, you're not going in there. Ms. Stephens told me that if you did not cooperate, I am to shoot you, wrap you in concrete and dump you in the river. I would enjoy killing you and I will. I just don't want all of the work associated with disposing of your sorry ass. Now get your shit and get out of here. I'm done asking."

Danny was not privy to Big D's secrets, but he had noticed that men who crossed him tended to disappear. He suspected that Billy Mac was capable of doing exactly what he was threatening. Danny was

drunk and high, but not ready to die. He gave Billy
Mac the keys, threw his belongings, the ones Danielle
let him have, in the old company pickup truck and left.

Billy Mac liked big women. One of his favorite
sayings was "there are two kinds of women, good ole
big ones and big ole good ones." If they had money,
all the better, he didn't really care about the money. As
Danny drove off, Billy Mac returned to the house.

On Monday morning Danielle met with Mary in
Big D's office which was, more and more, becoming
Danielle's office. Billy Mac had cleaned up the office
and had disposed of Hernandez, his accomplice, and
their car. The men had been put in the car, partially
covered with concrete, and in the dark of night
discreetly slipped from a barge into the deepest channel
of the Mississippi River. Billy Mac was proud of his
work. Danielle was pleased as well. She liked Billy
Mac. He was rough and ugly, but he was a real man,
nothing like her soon-to-be ex.

Billy Mac was now assigned to hang around the office building as a driver for Danielle. Danielle and Mary were certain that they had not heard the last from the Boss, whoever he was. The name of the Boss was one of the few things about Big D's business Mary did not know. She wondered out loud to Danielle if Big D himself knew the name.

There were other problems: the three ongoing projects, all losers without an infusion of money. Danielle expressed her concerns. "Mary, what can I do about the three projects? Should I put my money in them?"

"No Danielle, the FBI will be watching, and they will seize any unaccounted for money you try to sneak into the projects. The projects must stand on their own."

Danielle wanted to save the business. "I can't just close the business." She was thinking of her father's legacy. To Memphis as a whole, Big D was still a highly successful businessman. "Bankruptcy is not an option, my father's legacy and too many skeletons in the closets."

Mary had been thinking about the situation; she too wanted to save the business. "Look at the problem from the other side."

Danielle was already starting to see what Mary was thinking. "What do you mean?" She paused, thinking, "What would happen to our customers if we left them high and dry?"

"Exactly, the problem is not all yours. D-Line is on the contracts, not you. D-line has few assets; this building and the yard are mortgaged in excess of their value, and most of the equipment is rented. Unless your customers make concessions, D-Line can't complete the jobs. Two of the jobs are bonded. I bet the bonding companies could be talked into helping if they saw the condition of this company. Sell your Mercedes and Danny's Porsche, put your fancy jewelry and shoes away, and let's go talk to some people. "

Danielle could see this strategy working. "What if they put D-Line into involuntary bankruptcy?"

Mary had thought this through. "You must convince everyone that it is you who will put D-Line in bankruptcy if they don't make concessions. Your

lawyer from now on needs to be the bankruptcy
lawyer."

The plan could work. D-Line's customers, its
bank, and the bonding company had a lot more to lose
than did Danielle. Further, Danielle would see to it that
they would all underestimate her. She could put on the
big, spoiled, orphan act. It would not be hard; it was
exactly what they all already thought. The balancing
act would involve somehow convincing these people
that in spite of the known shortcomings, she was smart
enough to complete the jobs. That is where Mary
would come in.

It would be a high wire act with no net. Sure,
Danielle had a few hundred thousand dollars, but she
recognized that she could not live long on several
hundred thousand dollars. Her Mercedes and Danny's
Porsche alone cost that much. No, Danielle had to find
a way to earn some real money.

CHAPTER 14. *BIG MAMOU.* Link Davis

https://www.youtube.com/watch?v=Ss-pVsvcSpw

Cortez Castaneda was a first generation U.S. citizen. His parents had immigrated from Guatemala shortly before he was born in New Orleans. He was dark complexioned, with black hair, oiled, and slicked back. Cortez grew up in Kenner, Louisiana. School was "not his thing," so he quit in the 10th grade and got a job as a painter. Working for someone else was likewise "not his thing," and soon he was unemployed and making money selling drugs. This didn't work either, and before long, he was forced to join the Marines to avoid jail.

Cortez served his country with distinction, if not willingly. As soon as his enlistment was up, he left the service. Cortez still bore himself with the air of a Marine, just not with the honor. The Marines instilled a work ethic and pride in Cortez. When he left the Marines, he was smarter, more determined, and more focused.

After leaving the Marines, his family wanted him out of Kenner and away from the friends who had led him down the wrong path. To placate his family, Cortez settled with a cousin in Mamou, Louisiana, and started painting houses. Before long Cortez also had a part-time job selling drugs in the relatively small Latino community in and around nearby Opelousas and Lafayette.

Cortez was shrewd, worked hard and now had several legitimate, successful companies based out of Lafayette: a painting company, a landscaping company, and a roofing company. All of his companies employed Latino workers, some legal, but most not. Cortez could and did live well. He could have maintained his lifestyle with the profits generated by his legitimate businesses, but he was greedy, with a chip on his shoulder. So he continued with his illegal business and was now the most successful drug dealer in southwest Louisiana and into southeast Texas. Some of Cortez's customers called Cortez Slick, because of his slicked back hair. Cortez's employees called him Mr. Castaneda.

Unlike many drug dealers, Cortez was not particularly violent. He could be, but only when absolutely necessary. Virtually the only time Cortez resorted to violence would be to protect or avenge one of his employees or one of the Latino families, and the violence was almost always directed at a *gringo*. Cortez had the luxury of avoiding violence against his *people*, because so many of them were illegal immigrants, both his employees and his customers and he had developed an association, with several local customs agents. If an employee or even a customer caused any grief to Cortez, they would soon find themselves deported. The customs agents were pleased with the tips on where they could locate illegals and more so with the gifts from Cortez, which some might call bribes. It was a symbiotic, if not an altogether legal, relationship.

Cortez picked his drug dealers from the people employed in his legitimate businesses and had gradually insulated himself, with lieutenants, from those actual dealers. Castro Hernandez had been one such lieutenant.

Cortez had an office in the warehouse out of which he conducted his businesses. The office looked like any other office of a relatively small contractor. Cortez was careful not to draw attention to himself. He drove a five-year-old Chevy truck and lived in a modest neighborhood, mostly inhabited by other Lantinos. His house was larger than most, but inconspicuous. Few, if any, of his customer and neighbors knew about his villa near Quetzaltenango (Xela), Guatemala. Cortez was a cautious man.

In addition to his home in Guatemala, Cortez did allow himself some other luxuries. For instance, he liked Cuban cigars and Guatemalan rum. It was 7 pm and Cortez sat in his office smoking a Partagas cigar and sipping on Ron Zacapa rum. With him were two of his top lieutenants. The subject was the disappearance of Castro Hernandez. No one else was allowed to smoke anywhere in the building. The lieutenants were allowed a beer. Neither man talked; they knew better than to speak unless asked to do so.

Cortez addressed his men. "Any sign of Castro?"

One of the men answered. "I have asked everyone. No one has seen him since he left for Memphis."

"What about the car? Where is the car?" Cortez was clearly unsatisfied with what he was being told. He was looking at the second man.

The second man had to answer. "No sign of the car either. The man who was with Castro is also missing."

Carlos said to no one in particular. "Who's running Big D's business?"

No one answered. Cortez continued. "Castro told me that Big D's daughter was in the office and appeared to be in charge. From what he said she is nothing but a fat, spoiled brat. Castro never dealt with anyone but Big D. I don't know who has my money, but I intend to find out. Put a tail on the fat daughter. Find out where she goes. Find a place where I can meet her, alone. I think she knows more than she is saying, and find Castro—NOW."

CHAPTER 15. *OCCASIONAL WIFE.*
Faron Young

https://www.youtube.com/watch?v=uv5MyQrfc4g

Jen's mother at long last returned to Chalmette to live in the FEMA trailer. Jake moved back into the bedroom with Jen, because he gave her an ultimatum: he was either sleeping in the bedroom or back at the rental in Bossier City. That is not to say that all was fine with the Canes. Jen claimed to be trying but often suffered from morning sickness, or at least that was her excuse. Then there was his daughter, Eloise, who was going back and forth with her boyfriend, or as Jake called him, *"the sperm donor."*

The boyfriend wanted Eloise to move in with him in Dallas and promised that they would marry as soon as he graduated and was settled in a job. Jen was having none of it. She was against them living together and the promised marriage. Jake was caught in the middle. It seemed that no matter what he said about the relationship it was wrong, even if he thought he was agreeing.

Then there was Jubilee Jones. The search warrants had all been executed, and nothing had been found. Buddy, Jake, and Jen had all been summoned to meetings with Jubilee as had the Ebarbs. Nobody said anything on advice of counsel. That is to say, counsel for Jake, separate counsel for Jen, and separate counsel for the Ebarbs. Buddy choose to appear without representation.

Tim Barnette was afraid to represent Jake in case there was a conflict between Jake and Jen. Jake was forced to hire his own lawyer, a lawyer suggested by Tim, Harry Earl Pruett, better known as "Hoot." Tim referred to Hoot with reverence, for to Tim, Hoot was a real lawyer. On the golf course one Saturday morning, Jake asked Tim what he meant. Tim did not respond until they were in the bar alone after the round. "Jake, a real lawyer is willing into go into court and fight for his client."

Jake was confused. "I thought all of you represented people in court. That's what you do."

"No Jake, lawyers like me write contracts, write wills, handle successions, and advise people with their business deals. If my clients get in trouble, I find them a real lawyer."

Jake had known Tim for many years. "Don't give me that bull. You try cases. I know you have."

Tim had been drinking on the golf course and was by now slightly buzzed. That fact and the fact that he and Jake were longtime friends and business associates served to loosen Tim's tongue. "*Have*, is the operative word. I *have* tried cases and left pieces of me lying on the courtroom floor. I don't plan to try anymore cases. No, real lawyers like Hoot are the exception."

Jake was on his second beer. "If that's true, why are you representing Jen?"

"Jake, to start with, I don't have a clue about what you have gotten yourself into. No charges have been filed, for now I'm riding Hoot's coattails. If the shit hits the fan, Jen will need a real lawyer like Hoot. I'll find her one."

Jubilee was getting nowhere, and his star witness, in fact his only witness, Pinky, was now dead. Jubilee needed to shake things up. While he doubted that Jake and Buddy and the Ebarbs had anything to do with Pinky's death, they did have a motive. Jubilee arranged to meet with Hoot. They could speak the same language.

Harry Earl Pruett was the son of a Bossier Parish School teacher, a single mother. Hoot's father had left his wife years earlier and had left the state. Hoot knew where his father was, but had not seen him in over twenty years. Hoot grew up in Haughton, Louisiana, and graduated from Haughton High School. After high school, Hoot attended Northwestern State University in Natchitoches and then LSU law school on student loans and the money he earned clerking for a prominent criminal lawyer in downtown Baton Rouge. At no time did young Harry excel in school, but as a lawyer he quickly did. Hoot was short, had short man's disease, which he hid from nearly everyone. Hoot was always impeccably dressed. He had large ears that he hid under long graying hair. He remembered everyone he encountered. Knew all of the court personnel and most of the cops, and they all liked him. That was one of Hoot's assets. Everybody liked him and respected him, especially the local Judges, many of whose election campaigns had been bankrolled by Hoot and Hoot's friends.

The judges liked him for another reason: Hoot never appeared in court unprepared and never made an argument that was unsupported by the law. If he tried to extend the law in favor of his client, he was careful to explain to the judge the settled jurisprudence and his reasons for asking that it be extended to the facts before the court.

All of those attributes are important for a trial lawyer, but the most important thing, and the attribute Hoot had in spades, was the fact that he could talk to juries and make them like him, like his client, and forget that he was a lawyer. Hoot did not win every case; he lost a few, but won many. Because he would go to trial, appeared fearless and was effective, his guilty clients often obtained plea bargains far better than others.

When Hoot met with Jubilee, he had no idea why his client was the subject of a federal investigation. For that reason, a silk stocking corporate lawyer hired by Jake's firm accompanied Hoot to the meeting. Tim would not have respected the corporate lawyer. Hoot told the man that he was to say nothing. Hoot was pleasantly surprised when the lawyer abided by his request.

Jubilee spoke first. "Thank you for agreeing to this meeting, Mr. Pruett."

"Please call me Hoot, everybody does. May I call you Jubilee?" Hoot had done his homework. Most FBI agents were several grades more competent than the average city policeman. This agent was several grades higher than the average FBI agent. Hoot was anxious to learn why this agent was investigating his client.

"I will have a hard time calling a grown man Hoot, but I'll try. Hoot, I am sure that you know why we are targeting your client." Hoot didn't have a clue. There was some head movement, but he said nothing.

"I'm certain that your client is in possession of a large amount of drug money and a large amount of high grade heroin. I'm told that he has murdered one man, a Mario Prince, probably is an accessory to the murder of

Daniel Stephens, and may have had something to do with the murder of Sidney Jones. Your client is in deep trouble."

All of this was news to Hoot. His first thought was that he would need to renegotiate his retainer. His second thought was one of amazement. Hoot knew drug dealers and murderers. Jake Cane was neither. His third thought was, this guy has nothing but a theory; if he had any hard evidence, Jake would be in jail. The corporate lawyer was squirming, his breath noticeably quickened; Hoot made some unintelligible nod and said nothing.

Jubilee was not deceived. "I was wrong. I see that this is all news to you."

Hoot was impressed. He had maintained his best poker face, and this man had seen right through him. "Jubilee, my client has not been involved in any of the things you allege. What evidence of these things do you claim to have?" These rather direct words were delivered by Hoot in a tone that was decidedly non-confrontational.

"I am not at liberty to disclose that information at this time, Mr. Pruett."

Hoot remained silent, thinking: *back to Mr. Pruett, he has nothing.* "Then we have nothing more to talk about, do we."

Jubilee was not finished. "Your client is no career criminal. He is in more trouble than just me. Somebody is out a great deal of money and a huge amount of illicit drugs. That person or persons will come by to see your client, and he won't be carrying subpoenas."

"Are we done?" Hoot was calmly digesting what had just been said. If there was any truth to anything Jubilee had said, he was dead right about the people who claimed ownership of the money and drugs.

Hoot was not worried about the one thing that frightened him. The one thing that scared Hoot was to represent a client who had not committed the crime for which he was charged. No, Jubilee may not have the goods- yet, but he was not the kind to simply blow smoke up your ass. Jake might not be guilty of all of the crimes mentioned by Jubilee, but neither was he innocent.

Jubilee stood up and dismissed Hoot and the company lawyer. "For now, Mr. Pruett."

As they walked outside of the federal court house, the company lawyer commented. It was the first time he had spoken since entering the court house. "Do you think our client is innocent? I have met and talked to Jake. There is no way that he could have done those things."

Hoot was still taking it all in. "There is no such thing as an innocent client. My job is to keep him from being convicted."

CHAPTER 16. *LOUISIANA MAN.*
Rusty & Doug

https://www.youtube.com/watch?v=7cyk_g0cirA

Pougy Prejean and his mate, Miss T, lived outside of Point Barre, Louisiana, on the banks of Bayou Courtableau. Miss T worked part time at the Courtableau Seafood and Grocery where Pougy ran the chicken drop, a gambling game. The couple also hunted alligators, ran crawfish traps and even trapped nutria, depending on the season and the proximity of the game wardens. It was not a life for everyone, but Pougy and Miss T could not have been happier.

Things changed for the couple when Pougy happened upon an aluminum brief case hung up in some Cypress roots on the banks of the Atchafalaya River south of the Highway 190 Bridge. Whether the change would be for the better remained to be seen. Unbeknownst to Pougy, the case had been thrown into the river by Jake Cane on his trip back from his failed attempt to return the drugs to Kelley and Big D in New

Orleans. Pougy was now a small time drug dealer with a big time stash.

Pougy's clientele was limited to people he knew well. He didn't need a lot of money, so he only supplied a chosen few. Unfortunately, one of those few was a young fellow from Honduras who had been a customer of Cortez Castaneda. One of Cortez's dealers found out about the competition, told one of Cortez's lieutenants, who then told him.

Normally, Cortez would have called his friends at immigration and had Pougy deported. That easy solution was not available. Pougy and many generations before him were U.S. citizens. Cortez had other problems, namely the missing $800,000 he had used to stake Big D, so he delayed taking any action against Pougy, whom he saw as nothing more than a bother. Pougy was not selling to any of Cortez's other customers.

One night, not long after he had received the report about Pougy, Cortez woke up with an obvious question, a question he had heretofore overlooked. *Where was this Coon Ass getting his stash?* Cortez brooded the remainder of the night, *was some big dealer from New Orleans or Houston invading his territory?*

The next day Cortez called in the lieutenant in charge of that area of the state and instructed him to visit Pougy and find out just exactly where he was getting his drugs. Cortez also made it clear that Pougy was to be put out of business, one way or another.

The unfortunate man sent on this mission was Roberto Rodriguez, along with Cortez's local drug dealer, both illegal immigrants. The local dealer had done some checking and had learned the location of the fishing camp where Pougy and Miss T lived. He had also spied on the couple enough to see that, neither of them, posed much of a challenge. Miss T was five feet tall and weighed about a hundred pounds. Pougy was thicker and taller, but not by much. Roberto and the local dealer would get what they needed and, if necessary, dispose of the nuisance.

Late, under cover of a moonless, cloudy sky, the two approached Pougy's camp from opposite directions. Each of the men attracted the notice of neighborhood guard dogs. Undeterred, each moved closer to Pougy's home. Their simultaneous arrival was no surprise to the occupants.

After being visited by Pinky some months earlier, Miss T had replaced the bird shot in her shotgun with buckshot. Likewise, Pougy, now being wary of strangers, kept the rifle he often used to kill ensnared alligators within easy reach. The unsuspecting Roberto and his companion, rather than being the stalkers, turned out to be the prey.

As he approached the camp, Roberto was startled to hear a women's voice behind him. Miss T asked. "Who are you and what you doin' here?"

With that Roberto turned, revolver in hand, and fired in the direction from which the sound came. He only fired once, hitting the freezer Miss T was using as a shield. He probably never heard the report from Miss T's shotgun. Roberto was now feed for a family of alligators. The dealer fared no better. As soon as Pougy saw that the intruder was carrying a weapon, he shot the man squarely between his eyes.

The whole episode troubled Pougy and Miss T. Not so much the killings – anybody who was stupid enough to approach their home with a loaded weapon must have wanted to die. No, what troubled the couple was the question of why these two Mexicans were snooping around with guns? From across the bayou came a call. "What's going on over there?"

Pougy replied, hollering loud enough for all of his neighbors to hear, "A coyote was trying to get in my trash. He's alligator food now."

From down the bayou came a response, "Good. I have been trying to get that son of a bitch myself." With that the lights at the camps along Bayou Courtableau were gradually extinguished for the night.

Miss T was not happy. "Pougy, I told you that these drugs would bring us nothing but trouble. Get rid of them, now."

Pougy was busy loading Roberto in the boat. "Help me! This fellow is heavy."

Miss T lent a hand loading both men into Pougy's boat. "Pougy, I mean it, get rid of them drugs."

The next morning the first patrolman to arrive at the Port Barre Police department found an aluminum briefcase sitting by the backdoor. By the time Jubilee Jones and the FBI learned of the discovery, the drugs and the briefcase had been handled by every curious member of the Port Barre police force and by at least two Louisiana State Troopers. Or more correctly, as Jubilee would complain- mishandled. The only positive information the FBI was able to determine from a careful examination of the briefcase and its contents, was that the briefcase contained most of the heroin that had gone missing from the evidence room of the Tennessee Highway Patrol.

For his part, Cortez would soon find himself missing yet another of his lieutenants and one more of his dealers. Cortez resolved that he must take matters into his own hands. The little coon ass could wait; the fat bitch in Memphis owed him $800,000. He would deal with her first.

CHAPTER 17. *INVITAION TO THE BLUES.* James O'Gwynn

https://www.youtube.com/watch?v=kOYneP8KQyA

Jubilee was not the kind to get frustrated. He had that combination of persistence and patience that nearly always led to success- eventually. He sat pondering the fact that in spite of his best efforts, he had no hard evidence implicating Jake and Buddy with the shootout in Brownsville and none of his search warrants had turned up anything. What was worse, Hoot knew Jubilee had nothing. With no winning cards to play and nothing to scare his quarry into a mistake or into an admission, Jubilee was dead in the water.

Jubilee returned full time to his Memphis office. He did his best thinking behind his desk; surely the return to Memphis would provide the inspiration he so desperately needed. Fortunately, for Jake and Buddy, the return to the office had the opposite effect on the investigation. Jubilee had solved the murder of the senator's brother, the killer was dead, and the senator had returned to other matters. While, for political reasons, he would never admit as much, Senator Davis could have cared less about the shootout in Brownsville or any of the participants.

With no commands from above, Jubilee was expected to resume his duties as the Chief of the Memphis FBI office and to attend to the day to day operation of that office. These responsibilities had piled up in his absence. Jubilee was soon overwhelmed by other matters. For a while, at least, it appeared that Jake and Buddy were out of the woods.

At the same time, Danielle and Mary (Mary was now president and general manager of D-Line Construction) were trying to rebuild the company. Danielle had played her cards perfectly and had obtained concessions from all of her customers, her bank, and even from the bonding company. Harvey had been terminated and was now resting quietly at home. He had been replaced by a young woman with an MBA. The estimator for the company had also been terminated. The bonding company insisted on that move, and with the help of the bonding company, Mary had hired a seasoned estimator who wanted to slow down by working for a smaller company. D-Line was now showing a small profit on the existing jobs and had secured two new jobs which promised to be profitable.

Mary ran the office and Danielle, with the help of her "driver," Billy Mac, assumed supervision of the jobs. Danielle was a quick study; she only needed to hear something one time. More importantly, she had an uncanny ability to filter good information from bad. Employees and subcontractors alike soon learned that they better have their facts straight before they talked to Danielle. She had another important talent: she had the ability, like her father, to intimidate people. Danielle was smart, shrewd, and when necessary, downright mean. Normally, such qualities would hardly form the foundation for a loyal and productive workforce, but, in this case, it did. It is hard to conclude why it worked, but it did. Maybe it worked because the workers now saw their jobs as secure. Maybe it worked because while sometimes harsh, Danielle was fair and never favored anyone. Maybe it worked because the workers watched as Danielle asked intelligent questions, took good advice, and learned the construction business right before their eyes. Whatever, it was working. D-Line was becoming a legitimate construction company.

Never are times as good as they seem nor as bad as they seem. Danielle's situation was no different. With success came other problems. Danielle had at least two glaring problems. For one, her snot-nosed, soon to be ex-husband now claimed part ownership of the company. The other problem was that Billy Mac had noticed that they were being watched by at least one and maybe two different groups. If not for the second problem, Billy Mac would have quickly solved the first.

One of the groups of people watching Danielle was the FBI. Jubilee could not assign anyone full time to the job, but agents including Jubilee himself, were periodically watching Danielle, the company, and were monitoring the bank account for suspicious activity. The other group watching Danielle consisted of two men who worked for Cortez Castaneda, two men personally chosen by Cortez, two men who reported directly to Cortez.

One of Jubilee's agents noticed Cortez's men, and, with Jubilee's blessing, began to carefully monitor those men, which, at the same time allowed them to

keep tabs on Danielle. It was not that Cortez was
being irresponsible. How could Cortez know that
Danielle was under surveillance? Unfortunately the
men to whom Cortez had assigned the task were not
equipped to deal with the sophistication of the FBI.
Before long Jubilee had identified their employer and
the FBI office in Lafayette had begun an investigation
of a man heretofore unknown to anyone currently in
law enforcement.

Jubilee paid a visit to Danielle in her office. If
Danielle was concerned, she never showed it. "What
can I do for you, Mr. Jones? Should I have my lawyer
present?" She didn't want to involve her lawyer. She
could hardly afford to stay in business and also
continue to support her lawyer and his family. "I can't
imagine what I could tell you that you don't already
know. You have searched everything but the inside of
my butt."

"Ms. Stephens," Jubilee knew that she had
returned to her maiden name, "I am here mainly to talk,
but I may have a few questions. I am certain that your
father was engaged in drug trafficking. It appears to me

that you are attempting to run a legitimate construction business."

Danielle was glad for those comments and at the same time, even more cautious than she had been at the start of the conversation. "I seriously doubt that my father was involved in any illegal activity." She lied. "But, thank you for the judgment of me." Thinking, *be careful, he is up to something. He'll get nothing from me.*

"Ms. Stephens, do you know a man by the name of Cortez Castaneda?"

Danielle was puzzled, *who is Cortez Castaneda? Do I know a Cortez Castaneda? I wish I could ask Mary.* "I am afraid to answer, is this some kind of trick?"

Jubilee was so smooth, too smooth for Danielle's liking. "No trick. I doubt that you do know him, but I have to ask."

"Excuse me if I am over cautious, Mr. Jones. I do not recall anyone by that name."

Normally Jubilee would have asked to be called by his first name, but Danielle was probably too young to be calling Jubilee by his first name. "Do you know of any reason why people who work for that man would be following you?"

Yes she did. *Was Cortez Castaneda the "Boss"?* "No Mr. Jones, I have no idea. Why would someone be following me?"

Jubilee could see that she was lying. "If I am right about your father, it probably has something to do with the drug business." Jubilee was certain that she already knew as much. He needed to know how much.

"Mr. Jones, you're wrong about my Dad, and I am tired of your unsupported allegations."

"Ms. Stephens, just forget about whether I am right or wrong. Just indulge me while I engage in a little speculation."

Danielle had to be careful; she wanted to know more about this Castaneda guy, without implicating her father. "I've got a little time, and I love a good story. My dad always told me that a story doesn't have to be true to be good."

Good Jubilee thought. "Okay, let's just suppose that a drug dealer became aware of an opportunity to buy a large quantity of high-grade heroin at a bargain price. Assume with me that this deal could result in a huge quick profit, but required more cash than was readily available to the drug dealer. Suppose that the drug dealer took on a silent partner, one who had access to a large amount of cash."

Danielle listened, realizing that Jubilee knew way more than she had imagined. "I can see where this fantasy is going."

Jubilee always let others talk, if he could. "Tell me. Complete the story for me."

"Sure, the dealer borrows the money. The deal goes bad, and he loses the money. Now the man he borrowed the money from wants his money back, and your imaginary drug dealer can't pay off the loan." Danielle was shrewd enough not to complete the story as it actually unfolded. "Are you telling me that my dad was murdered because he could not pay back a loan?"

For an instant, this conclusion surprised Jubilee. He now looked at Danielle with some grudging admiration. Not that he was buying her sincerity, but he had to admit that she was a clever one. "Well, it could have happened for that reason. Do you think that is what happened? Who was the person who lent your dad the money?"

Danielle had said enough. "It's your story. You made it up, not me. I don't believe any of it."

"Danielle, it's not fiction. It happened, and I think Cortez Castaneda is the man who was in business with your father or, at least funded the drug deal, but I don't think he killed your dad."

Danielle listened, trying not to act too concerned or too interested. "Okay, I'll play along, if this Castaneda guy didn't kill my father, who did?"

Jubilee did not hesitate. "I can't be certain, but I believe that a man by the name of Mathew Hawkins is likely the person who shot your father."

Danielle had to process this new bit of information. "Who is that? I've never heard of anyone by that name." She wanted to tell Jubilee about James Cane, but that would be revealing too much.

Jubilee continued. "Mathew Hawkins is an associate of James Cane. From my investigation, I have learned that he and James Cane probably have the drugs and money involved in the drug deal that went bad. The drug deal where two of your father's employees were killed."

Danielle took a moment to process what she heard. *So I can pretty much forget about getting the money from Cane. There are probably more FBI agents watching him than there are watching me.* After an uncomfortably long pause Danielle replied. "Why are you telling me all of this?"

Jubilee now knew he could rely on Danielle to help him. She would want to punish her father's killer. "Because I think you can help me to convict Hawkins and Cane of your father's murder."

Danielle was hooked, but she tried to pretend that she wasn't. "I'm not going to admit for one second that my father was involved in any illegal activity, whatsoever."

"I am not asking you to admit anything. Just help me trap the men who were responsible for your father's death."

After a short pause, Danielle responded. "I will help you on one condition."

Jubilee was a little taken aback. He thought he had her, but by now Danielle and Mary had realized that there was potential tax liability for the unreported cash the FBI. had discovered in auditing D-Line's construction projects. "Mr. Jones, if you pursue the potential tax liens against D-Line, I will be forced to close the business. I will help you, but only if you will promise to drop any attempt to collect past unpaid taxes."

Jubilee was a little embarrassed, but he hid it. In his zeal to get Jake, he had overlooked that problem. He had not yet shared his findings with the IRS. He knew that the business could never pay the tax. Had he thought about it and had he known that Danielle wanted to save the business, he might have used the threat of tax liens as leverage to obtain Danielle's help. Now he would, "If you cooperate with me fully, I will see that the tax liability is forgiven."

He now obtained the response he had so carefully sought. "What do you want me to do, Mr. Jones?"

CHAPTER 18. *I'M WALKING THE DOG.*
Webb Pierce

https://www.youtube.com/watch?v=J2cbkVZgUko

Jake and Buddy were sitting on the porch of the camp drinking whiskey. Maker's Mark with a little water and ice. They had spent the day with other members of the loosely organized "Duck Balls Hunting Club." Everyone but Jake and Buddy had gone home. The day had been spent getting the camp ready for hunting season, repairing deer stands, bush hogging trails, and generally fixing everything that needed fixing. Jake enjoyed these tasks. He enjoyed them more than he did the hunting. Jake was now in the best shape of his life, but for the extra drinking. He now worked out religiously in a program that was not unlike modern CrossFit. He was even attending a self-defense course. The workouts had the dual purpose of releasing stress and, Jake thought, preparing him for the next unwanted visitor.

Jake was explaining to Buddy why he would need to skip hunting on opening day. He would need to stay at the camp so that he could prepare the gumbo the

other members would enjoy for lunch. Opening day
was not far off. "Buddy, with Pinky dead, do you think
Jubilee is finally done with us?" Jake wanted an
answer he knew he would not receive.

Buddy decided to be gentle. "Did you notice
the two assholes in the Dodge pickup I chased off of
our lease this afternoon? Claimed to be lost. They
weren't lost. They were FBI agents spying on us. No,
Jubilee is not one to give up. He is not done."

Jake was not surprised. "I was wanting a
different answer. I thought those guys were out of
place out here. I was careful to stay away from the old
well. Do you think they could locate it from the air?"

"Jake, let's hope not. I guess you saw the
helicopter fly over yesterday."

The steaks were marinating at room
temperature, the coals on the charcoal grill were almost
ready, and the potatoes were done. Buddy and Jake
were planning on eating dinner, watching LSU on the
TV at Jake's not-so-rustic camp, and enjoying a quiet
night alone. Jen did not complain when Jake was gone.
Jake hated the fact that she did not complain.

Jake was thinking about his wife. He could not and would not discuss his wife with Buddy. Jake was deep in thought when he felt a cold nose nuzzle his left hand. Buddy had seen the dog approach. Jake had not and almost jumped off of the porch, spilling his drink in the process. The dog just looked on with curiosity, not the least bit spooked.

"Buddy, where did this raggedy mutt come from?"

"Beats me, she came from the direction of Lake Ivan. I think I saw her over in that direction earlier today."

The dog had the face of a poodle with curly black poodle hair and the body of a pit bull. Her hair was matted. She was skinny, malnourished, starving. She may have weighed thirty-five pounds and should have weighed fifty or sixty. She appeared to be a pup, one that on her best day would be ugly, but in her current condition, she bordered on disgusting. If ever a dog needed a friend, it was this poor girl. The dog ignored Buddy and fixated on Jake.

Jake wiped the remainder of his drink from the front of his dirty shirt and pants. "What are we going to do with this girl?"

"Jake, it's you that she likes, not me. What are you going to do with her?"

The dog was engrossed with Jake. "First, I'm going to get her some food." Neither Jake nor Buddy had a hunting dog, but other members of the club did, and there was a container of dog food inside, in the pantry. Jake found the food, a water bowl, and some dog shampoo. Jake said to no one, with Buddy sitting right in front of him, "This dog needs a name."

Buddy just watched. "Do you think Jen will let that dog into her house?"

Jake was silently considering just that fact. "She'd better. She's just a mutt herself; admittedly a much better looking mutt, but a mutt nonetheless."

Buddy wanted to name the dog "Pitdle" because she looked like a cross between a Poodle and a Pitbull, an idea promptly rejected by Jake. "Pitdle is what she will do on one of Jen's prized Oriental rugs." Jake seemed to be relishing the thought.

After dinner, "Princess Ivana," so named by Jake, suffered through a bath and an amateur haircut to remove a few of the larger mats of hair, and was rewarded with a steak bone which she accepted with unconcealed glee. That night and every night for the rest of her life Princess slept inside, this night on some other dog's bed. Afterwards, she was rarely out of Jake's sight. She absolutely and visibly adored Jake, followed him everywhere, went everywhere with him and was a fixture in his office.

At first, Jen was secretly jealous of Princess and wondered if Jake would care as much for anything else. Next to Jake, Princess grew to love Jen almost as much and eventually won her over. In the process the dog somehow imperceptibly healed the rift between Jake and Jen. Jake often said that the dog was the second best thing that ever happened to him. Marrying Jen was the first.

The dog was loyal, affectionate, and protective. In days shortly after she moved to the Cane's luxurious home, the Canes felt at times that she might be a little overly protective. That opinion was destined to change.

CHAPTER 19. *TROUBLE'S BACK IN TOWN.* William Brothers

https://www.youtube.com/watch?v=zsfefmPRADQ

Kelley had no trouble ditching the surveillance, nor was it difficult to disable the tracking device that had been surreptitiously affixed to the frame of his car. On his last visit to Shreveport he had borrowed a car. This time he would take his own BMW. He was not going to do anything illegal. He just needed to check with Jake, confirm that his money was still safe, and find out when the money would be available. He told Jackie that he had to visit an old friend. She was suspicious but had not questioned him.

The trip to Shreveport was pleasant and uneventful. The BMW was built for long trips, so the trip was easy. On the road, Kelley thought about how he could meet with Jake without being seen by the authorities. He was amused by the realization that after so many years of being the police, he was now the target. Not to worry, he knew the ways of the authorities; he knew their ways better than they did.

It was early afternoon when Kelley arrived in Shreveport. He had a prepaid cell phone, but he worried that Jake's phones might be tapped. He called Jake at the office. "May I speak to Jake? This is Buddy."

The receptionist buzzed Jake. "Buddy's on line 3." Buddy never called Jake at the office; she did not recognize the voice.

Jake was caught off guard, *why would Buddy be calling him at work? Why would Buddy call at all in the middle of the day? It must be important.* Without thinking it through, Jake picked up the line. "Hey, Buddy. What's going on?"

Kelley replied. "Can you meet me behind the Barnwell on the river front? I just got me a dog and you will love him."

The voice on the line was not Buddy's, of that Jake was certain. The voice was only slightly familiar. The accent? On the phone he could hear a twang like that of one of his clients from Arkansas. Then it hit him- Kelley. "Sure, I want to see the dog, but I'm working now." *Why is Kelley here?* He was perhaps the last person Jake wanted to see. Jake started to think. *If his lines were being monitored, time was important. If he goes now, he may be able to meet with Kelley, find out what he wants, and be gone before the FBI can get someone to check out the call.* That was exactly what Kelley was thinking. Jake replied. "Let me shut down my computer, and I'll be right there."

To Jake's surprise Kelley did have a dog. It was a German Sheppard pup, the offspring of Kelley's dog, Kaiser. The dog was for K J. Kelley brought the dog with him for company. "Hello, Jake. Meet Katrina K.J.'s new dog. She has been tearing up everything and pissing everywhere. Couldn't leave her at home unattended, so I brought her with me. Turns out she likes to travel. She's beautiful, isn't she?"

Jake was pretty certain that Kelley had more to talk about than this rambunctious puppy. "She is a handsome dog. Why are you here, Kelley? It could be bad for us both to be seen together."

Kelley and Katrina started walking down the bike trail that runs along the Red River. He motioned to Jake. "Let's walk and talk."

Jake was not exactly dressed for a walk. At least he had left his coat and tie at the office. "What do you want to talk about?" As if he didn't know, money was what he wanted to talk about.

Kelley replied on cue. "When am I going to get the money?"

"Kelley, we can go get the money now if you want it, I am past ready to get rid of it."

Kelley noticed the car first. It was a plain dark grey Chevy Impala. Inside were two men in grey suits, one held a camera with a telephoto zoom lens. If Kelley could have seen his BMW, he would have seen two similarly attired men snooping around. "Jake, I don't think I want the money right now." Nodding toward the Chevy now parked along Clyde Fant Parkway.

Jake had seen such men snooping about, just not recently. "I thought they had gone on to other things. I wonder how they got here so quickly? Were you followed? Do you think they are listening to our conversation?"

"I wasn't followed. I don't see a listening device, unless you are wired." Kelley expertly and quickly frisked Jake.

"That's smart, Kelley. Now they have a picture of us hugging."

Kelley was satisfied that Jake was not wired. "What's the difference? They have no evidence, just theories and speculation. They will call us in and neither of us will tell them anything. It's not good, but it is not the worst thing that could have happened. They should have waited until you gave me the money."

"When will this be over?" Jake thought out loud. Then added. "Goodbye, I must go make an appointment with my lawyer. He is having a very good year, and it keeps getting better, and say hello to Jubilee when you get home."

The sarcasm was not lost on Kelley as they parted ways. "Jubilee, that son-of-a-bitch, why won't he just give up?"

Jake left work early and went by Buddy's shop. FBI in tow. It was still safe to talk in Buddy's shop, he made certain of that fact. Jake asked Buddy to step outside and made a show of pointing out the surveillance team parked across the street. Back in the shop Buddy listened politely and carefully to the story.

When Jake was finished, Buddy spoke, as if to no one in particular. "You say it was no more than thirty minutes between receiving the call and your meeting with Kelley. There is no way they were able to intercept the call, digest it and have agents on site in that short amount of time. They are watching us, but they don't have people with us twenty-four hours a day. Was Kelley in his own car?"

"Yeah, he was, but he had disabled the tracking device."

Buddy was thinking. *I'm sure that he did, disable* one *of the tracking devices, I bet they concealed a second one. Kelley is not as smart as he thinks he is. I wish I still had inside information. As soon as we got hot, my sources dried up. Not that I would put them in jeopardy by asking anything anyway.*

Buddy continued, "Kelley knew better, he must be getting desperate. I bet that woman is putting pressure on him. I bet she wants to go home. He must actually love her-- that will get you in trouble every time."

Jake was not going to touch that last observation. Buddy's latest girlfriend had already gotten fed up and had moved on. Buddy would never let them get close. Instead Jake changed the subject. "I have an appointment with Hoot tomorrow. I bet we'll be visiting Jubilee again."

Buddy replied as Jake was leaving, "So will Kelley. His amnesia ruse is wearing kinda thin. Is he smart enough to keep his mouth shut?"

Jake answered without conviction. "I hope so."

CHAPTER 20. *HE'LL HAVE TO GO.*
Jim Reeves

https://www.youtube.com/watch?v=bpi8Bek6jdM

Danny Gentry was not a happy man. Not until after Danielle kicked him out did he realize just how good his life had been. No longer the manager of Platinum Plus and worse yet excluded, he was not even allowed in the bar he had recently managed. He was out of work, out of money, and living in his parent's basement. Worse still, he was equally unwelcomed by his soon to be ex-wife and by his parents, who were demanding that he get a job and his own place to live. The marriage contract he had signed at the behest of his mother turned out to be yet another bad idea. Everything he thought he owned with Danielle, including the house in the Cooper-Young neighborhood, turned out, were in her name, her separate property.

Danny called Danielle planning to unleash all of his charms and good looks. He had to get her back. Danny did not see himself driving an old work truck for long, and he was just smart enough to recognize that he was not going to live in the manner in which he had been accustomed on the basis of his own skills. Problem was, Danielle would not take his calls, and Billy Mac was always with her. *Driver my ass, drive her was more like it.*

Danny was just dumb enough to believe that he had something Danielle wanted, needed. In reality, he never had anything to offer and now that she had Billy Mac as her "driver," Danielle was well aware of that fact. Danny would not face the facts and had convinced himself that if he could get to Danielle, she would recognize that he was the catch he saw himself to be.

There was only one regularly, scheduled time when Danielle went out without Billy Mac – Wednesday happy hour with a group of girls all about her age. The girls usually met at Bosco's or at the Young Avenue Deli for drinks and gossip. The get-together, unofficially dubbed, "Wet Wednesday," lasted an hour or two at the most. There was plenty for the girls to discuss: jobs, boyfriends, ex-boyfriends, husbands, ex-husbands, and even children. Danielle seldom missed "Wet Wednesday." Especially with all of the rumors that concerned Danielle, to miss would allow open season on Danielle, her business, and her father. Danny knew about "Wet Wednesday" and had decided that he would casually show up at about the time when the meeting normally adjourned and unleash all of his charms on his wife.

When Danny entered the bar, he took no notice of the three swarthy men sitting near the door. Had he seen these men, he might have thought that they were mismatched and out of place. One of the men stood out. He was of average size but clearly overdressed with black polished pointy-toed shoes and a shiny black suit. He wore a grey-checked shirt with a gold chain around his neck. His hair was jet black and slicked back. Anyone who observed the men could have quickly gleaned that this man was in charge. He had an air about him, an incongruous military bearing. The two men with him did not initiate any of the conversation, what little there was. They just sat, menacingly silent.

A careful observer might also have noticed other people in the bar who were out of place. These people were not sitting together and were careful to make infrequent eye contact. One of these people was a thirty-something aged man who sat in a corner nursing a beer. A masculine, also thirty-something woman was sipping on a glass of iced tea in another corner. The third person did blend in. He was a somewhat older black man in cheap gray pants, a short-sleeved white shirt, and a blue blazer from JC Penney's. This man was visiting with a couple, but after Danny sat down at the bar, he casually moved next to Danny. He was sipping on what appeared to be some kind of mixed drink.

Danny took no notice of any of this as he sat alone waiting for an opening. Danielle had not seen Danny. "Wet Wednesday" was winding down. As Danielle started to leave, she focused on the group of men near the door and at the same time Danny, who was leaving his perch at the bar and was moving toward her. Danielle was wondering: *What the hell is he doing here?* Before she could react to Danny, one of the swarthy men stepped in front of Danielle and asked her if she would join his group for a drink.

Danny did not get far. The man sitting next to him stopped his progress. Jubilee spoke forcefully, a little out of character. "Sit back down, Danny, and let me buy you another beer." With that Jubilee made a point of nonchalantly allowing his coat to open revealing his badge and the pistol holstered under his coat. Danny started to say something, but before he could, Jubilee spoke again, now revealing his engaging personality. "You don't want to mess with those fellows (nodding at Slick and company). They might just kill you. Just sit back down and let's talk."

Danny sat down. "Who are you?"

Jubilee spoke without emotion. "FBI Special Agent Jubilee Jones. If you want to stay healthy and free, you'll do as I say. I have a video of you purchasing cocaine outside of Platinum Plus, and if you move, I will arrest you, you will go to jail, and you will stay in jail for a long time."

Danny now recognized one of the other FBI agents sitting in the back corner sipping on a beer; he had seen the same man at Platinum Plus. Danny sat down and accepted the beer. Jubilee positioned himself so that as he talked to Danny, he could observe the table where Slick sat quietly. Nothing further passed between the men about the cocaine, the only feature of the situation that was a relief to Danny.

The man who had approached Danielle spoke with an accent. "Danielle Stephens?... My boss wants to talk to you. Will you sit with us for a minute?" This man also flashed a gun hidden under his coat.

Danielle knew that she could not be so easily enticed if she were going to accomplish her mission. "I will not. Who the hell are you? What do you want?"

The man was undeterred. "My boss just wants to talk. If we meant you any harm, we would not have approached you in a public place."

Danielle persisted, "You didn't tell me who you are. Why would I want to talk to you?"

By now they were adjacent to the table where Cortez had been seated. He stood erect like a soldier as they approached. "My name is Cortez Castaneda. You don't know me, but I was an associate of your father. Will you allow me a few moments of your time?"

Danielle reached for her car keys in her purse while simultaneously switching on the microphone embedded in the lining. "How did you know my dad? I never heard him mention your name."

Castaneda was calm. He spoke in a soothing tone. "Did he ever mention Castro Hernandez?"

"I think he did one time. He may have had some business dealings with that man. That's all I know. What does Castro Hernandez have to do with any of this? I've got to go, I don't know anything about you, and I don't know anything about any Castro Hernandez." Danielle was playing her part to perfection and she knew it.

Castaneda was watching her closely. He was certain that Danielle knew something. "Danielle, you can sit down and talk, or you can spend the rest of what promises to be a short life looking over your shoulder for one of my friends." He gestured toward the two men with him.

Danielle feigned a bit of fear. She sat down next to Castaneda. "Okay, tell me how you know my father and make it quick."

Castaneda continued. "Through my employee, I staked your father with $800,000 and I want it back. I have been watching you, and I fear that you do not have the money."

"Mr. Castaneda, you are right about one thing, I don't have $800,000. I gave Castro all of the money I could find, less than $100,000. Ask him, he got all of the money my dad left."

Castaneda thought for a minute. *Had Castro run off with my money, where was he? I'll find him and deal with him later.* "So you do know Castro. This is not the first you have heard about this."

Danielle had to string this out. Jubilee told her what to say, but it was up to her to be convincing. "No, it is not. How do I know who you are? How do I know that you are not just one of a succession of hoodlums who will continue to harass me for the rest of my life?"

Castaneda instinctively knew that she had the information he wanted. "You will need to use your intuition. I am the man, and you know it. You know where the money is, don't you?"

Danielle paused. "I don't know that anyone gave my father $800,000. That's what Castro said; that's all I know about any $800,000. That and the fact that I don't have the money."

Castaneda could tell he was getting close. "Castro did give your father the money. My cousin was with him when he did. The money was mine. Where is it?"

"I'm not saying that I know, but if I did, and if I tell you, will you and Castro go away and leave me alone?"

Castaneda would have promised anything. "Tell me what you know and you will never hear from me again."

Danielle waited several heartbeats before she answered. "I am just a kid. My dad is dead, and all he left me was a failing construction company and this shit."

He had her. "You must trust me. Tell me what you know and I'm history."

Danielle had played as long as she dared. "I don't have the money, but I think I know who does. If I tell you, will you leave me alone?"

This statement was not exactly what Castaneda was expecting. He studied Danielle for any signal that she was lying. "Did you tell this to Castro?"

Danielle appeared to be telling the truth. "No, I never told him anything. I denied having any knowledge of any of this, which was true at the time. He told me that he would report to his boss and that he would be back. I assume he told you all of this. After he left, I did some checking around and figured out the name of the person with your money."

Castaneda was suspicious. It pays to be suspicious in his line of work. "Tell me more."

"I didn't know anything about my father being involved with any drug deals. Having studied the books of the construction company, I found unexplained cash infusions that kept the business running. He seems to have been laundering money through the business. After he left, I wondered if Castro really had provided money to my dad. It made some sense, since two of our employees were killed in a shootout in Brownsville, Tennessee, several months ago."

All of this was being recorded on a device concealed in the purse of the female agent seated nearby. Castaneda was oblivious and determined. "Where is the money?"

"My dad somehow found out that a man in Shreveport took the money and drugs after the shootout. My dad was in New Orleans to retrieve the money and drugs when he was killed. I think the man from Shreveport killed my father."

Was this too easy? Castaneda was guarded. The bitch had already said that she found about this after she met with Castro. "How did you find out all of this?"

Danielle did not hesitate. "I found out through my wormy little bookkeeper."

Castaneda had actually thought about talking to Harvey, the bookkeeper, but had learned that he had been institutionalized. Castaneda had his doubts that Big D would have confided in that little wimp. "Are you saying that your dad told Harvey Nelson about all of this?"

Danielle now went back to the script. "Not exactly. What I found out was that my dad told Harvey to find out everything he could about a man in Shreveport. Dad told Harvey that the man owed the company a lot of money. Later my dad told Harvey that he was going to New Orleans to collect the money the man owed him. After being accosted by your man Castro, I put two and two together. That man killed my father, I hope you get your money back and I hope you kill that bastard in the process."

Castaneda was quiet, thinking the story made sense and it was all he had. "Who is this mystery man?"

Danielle now told the truth as she knew it. "His name is James Cane. He is a stockbroker with a big firm in Shreveport. He is all over the Internet. I've looked. Extraordinarily successful in business. Seems to be happily married with two nearly grown children. Does not seem like the kind of person who would get involved in this kind of thing."

Castaneda had been around enough to know that appearances can be deceptive. He thought himself to have been successful at deception. "You think that this person killed your father?"

"Yes I do, but for another reason, something my dad said to me. He was vague, but I took from his comments that he had sent two men to Shreveport to collect a debt, and only one of them had returned. He never said exactly, but he indicated that one of them had been murdered. I was there for my allowance. I now wish I had listened more carefully and had asked some questions. Every day I wish that I had paid more attention to things my dad told me." Danielle wiped a real tear from her eye as she continued, "I have studied the books. Our company never did any work in Shreveport, and no one in Shreveport owed our company any money. Nowhere in any of our records does the name "James Cane" appear. We don't have any drugs and your man Castro took what little money we had. If my father ever had your money, we don't have it now. If I were looking for the money, I'd ask James Cane."

Castaneda was skeptical, but he had nothing else. He was certain that Danielle did not have the drugs and money. "You better be right, or I'll be back."

Danielle did not even bother to remind him that he had promised to leave her alone if she would tell him what she knew. She was growing up fast. She had never believed Castaneda for a second. Her trust was in Jubilee Jones, and if Jubilee didn't solve her problems, perhaps Billy Mac could.

As she left, Danielle glanced toward Jubilee and saw again her punk-ass, soon to be ex-husband. Her dad had warned her about Danny. Again she missed her dad and wished she had listened to his advice and moreover, wished he were still here. If Big D were alive, Danielle told herself, none of these problems would exist.

CHAPTER 21. *PLASTIC SADDLE.*
Nat Stuckey

https://www.youtube.com/watch?v=D-AAb3RbCs0

The next morning, Jake told Jen about the visit from Kelley, expecting to get, at best, a lecture about stupidity. Instead she listened silently to the whole story without comment. When she did speak, to Jake's surprise, she blamed Kelley, not Jake. "Kelley must really be brain damaged. Why would he do such a thing? Have you told Hoot? You will likely be visiting with Jubilee again. "

Jake was drinking coffee in their kitchen, with Princess sitting at his feet. His mother-in-law was back in Chalmette, and but for Kelley's visit, life was as normal for Jake as it had been in months. "I have an appointment with Hoot this afternoon. I had deluded myself into thinking that this was all passing. When will all this end?"

Jen changed the subject. "John came by yesterday to see Eloise."

For a second Jake was lost, *John who*? Then it hit him, John, the sperm donor, his daughter's erstwhile boyfriend. "What's he doing here? I see that he managed to avoid me."

"Jake, my dad accepted you. Give John a chance. He wants to meet you for lunch today. Cancel any plans you have and meet him at the Shreveport Club at noon." It was an order, not a request, and Jen seldom put anything in the form of an order.

Jake caught himself before he blew up and said: *All I need today is more drama.* Instead Jake answered. "Okay, any idea what he wants to talk about?" Whatever it was, Jake was certain that he was not the least bit interested.

Jen calmly replied. "He wants to marry Eloise and he wants your approval."

"Does he get it?" Jake replied. It was Jen's approval that was important, and there was no need to pretend otherwise. In Jake's view the kid was not all bad and he didn't totally blame the pregnancy on John. In fact, although he never said it out loud, he blamed the pregnancy, both pregnancies on the women.

"That's up to you Jake."

So you say, he started to say but caught himself again. He silently congratulated himself, *I'm getting better at this marriage thing.* "What do you think?"

Jen replied. "He's a good kid. I think we should give him a chance."

Again, Jake had a thought, but kept it to himself: *Yeah, I don't want any little bastards running around the house either.* "I'll give my assent, but not before I make him suffer."

Jen seemed pleased. "Thanks. We need to plan a wedding and soon." Jen was barely showing, but Eloise was not. Jen knew that everyone would be counting the months. She didn't care. Her daughter was going to have the wedding she had wanted for herself, whether she wanted it or not. "I have checked around, and all of the venues for a reception are booked."

Jake sat quietly drinking his coffee. Jen was not expecting an answer. Jake had learned, somehow, that important lesson. The husband cannot fix everything, and the wife does not expect him to. Jen would find a venue. She did not need or want Jake's help. All that was required of him was to listen or at least pretend to listen.

The meeting with John went well. Just a scared kid about to find his life ruled by two strong-willed Cane women. The only promise Jake required from John was that he not interfere in any manner with the wedding preparations or the wedding itself. John was bewildered by that request. He had naively thought they would simply marry before a justice of the peace, move in together, and that would be it. Jake explained to John. "A lot of things in your life are about to change. Embrace the changes and enjoy the journey." Jake continued. "Before you accept something for nothing, think about the consequences. Nothing is free." John had no idea what that comment was about. He just let it go and finished his lunch. He would have to learn the hard way like everyone else.

The meeting with Hoot that afternoon went as well as could be expected. Hoot was not as understanding as Jen had been. "Why in God's name would you agree to meet with Kelley?" Hoot now knew a few of the details concerning Jake's "problem," as little of the details as Hoot thought he needed to know. He knew who Kelley was, and he was pissed. "How can I keep you out of jail if you act like some kind of cowboy and go off halfcocked without contacting me? Do you think you are bulletproof with your money and reputation? Well, you are not. Bringing down a man of your wealth and position in the community is what those snot-nosed prosecutors live for. Your kind are trophies. There is nothing they would enjoy more than hanging your head on their office wall. The guilty verdict in your case will be framed. For years the details of the trial will be talked about at the meeting of prosecutors."

Jake interrupted. "Okay, I get it, it won't happen again. What's done is done. What can we do now?"

Hoot calmed down. "First, you can pay me another $10,000."

Jake was as used to that request as he could get. Too bad he couldn't access the money that was the root of the "problem." "That's a big surprise. Then what?"

"Jubilee has already called. He is flying down tomorrow. He wants to meet with us at the FBI office tomorrow afternoon. I told him that I will be there, but you're not coming without a subpoena and even with a subpoena, I will instruct you to exercise your right to remain silent."

Jake got up to leave. Every minute was costing him money. "Let me know what he says. He's got nothing. So what if I run into a guy with a dog on the riverfront. What does that prove?"

Hoot was not as confident. "You ever hear about 'circumstantial evidence'? By itself, you're right, it proves nothing, but enough coincidences could land your ass in jail, and you would not fare well in jail."

"I'll have a $10,000 check delivered to you this afternoon. For that, I trust you can keep me out of jail until after the wedding." Hoot did not respond. By the time Hoot computed the last statement Jake was gone. *What wedding?*

That night Jen informed Jake that the rushed wedding would be held at the First Methodist Church in three weeks, stuck in between two other weddings. The reception would be held at The Municipal Auditorium, formerly the home of The Louisiana Hayride. Jake approved, as if it mattered. His father would have also approved. The venue might just be the Cradle of another Star, Jake's unborn grandson.

CHAPTER 22. *JOLE BLON.* Doug Kershaw, Jimmmy C. Newman, Jo-El Sonnier

https://www.youtube.com/watch?v=HbfYaSkPm44

Jake and several friends were drinking and having dinner at the Petroleum Club, ostensibly discussing a benefit function for a city council member. They were enjoying themselves a little too much. A few had already answered or ignored cell phone calls from worried or angry wives. It was time to go, but it was a good group, and only a few had left to catcalls from the rest.

Jake's phone rang, it was the ring tone reserved for Jen. "Jake, we have had visitors, some of your friends, no doubt. Thank god for Princess. Come home now."

Jen was obviously distraught, and Jake did not hesitate. "Are you okay?"

"I'm okay, they won't be coming back, but the police are coming. I can hear the sirens. The neighbors must have heard the gunshots and called. Come home now."

"I'll be home as soon as I can get there." Jake responded as the phone went dead.

When Jake arrived home, the police were already talking to Jen. He could see nothing out of place at first. In fact, he saw nothing out of place until one of the police officers pointed out the several pieces of torn cloth strewn about his front lawn and Princess angrily tearing at what appeared to have recently been an expensive shoe. One of the other policemen, a woman, was holding a semi-automatic pistol with her pencil. He did not recognize the make. One thing was certain; the gun did not belong to the Canes. Jake decided to remain silent. As Jen talked to the patrol officer; Jake called Hoot.

Hoot did not give out his cell phone number to anyone. That is to anyone but Jake. After the encounter with Kelley, Jake had demanded the number before paying the additional retainer. Hoot was pleasant. It was the first time Jake had called Hoot on the cell phone.

Jake had suspected that there had been a visit from someone wanting the money and the heroin. It was becoming a trend. Jake said to Hoot. "I really don't know what happened. I decided to call you first and ask questions later or better yet let you ask the questions."

Hoot's reply should not have surprised Jake. "First, you say nothing to anyone, especially the police. Tell me what you do know."

"Something has happened at my house. I just got home. Jen is talking to the police. All I know is that there has been gunfire, torn clothes, and a gun I do not recognize. Princess is ripping up someone's expensive shoe."

"Who the hell is Princess?" Hoot was worried. Jubilee was right. Someone was coming for the drugs and the money. "Tell Jen to clam up and then call Tim. I will be talking to Tim. If the line is busy, tell her to keep trying."

By the time the detective had arrived, Jen was "unable" to give a statement. Jake explained to the detective that she was too distressed and pregnant on top of all else. "Can you come back later?"

The police were still present when Tim arrived, followed shortly by Hoot. Neither was accustomed to making house calls.

The detective immediately recognized Hoot. "What are you doing here, Hoot?" She looked at Tim as she spoke to Hoot. Tim looked vaguely familiar.

Hoot answered, "Friend of the family. What happened?"

The detective secretly had the hots for Hoot. She was more than willing to have a conversation with him. "Two men in a silver sedan accosted Mrs. Cane. They asked for Mr. Cane. He was not home. It is not clear what they were after. Mrs. Cane thinks that they may have been Hispanic."

Hoot continued to listen. Tim kept quiet. "What's with the torn cloth?" Hoot could now see blood on the cloth and a trail of blood on the grass. "Did someone get shot?" As he looked around he noticed Princess still ripping up a shoe. *So, Princess is a dog.*

The detective was full of information. "I don't know if anyone was shot. Mrs. Cane is not injured. Her dog apparently attacked the intruder, and Mrs. Cane ended up with his gun. (She nodded at the semi-automatic pistol now lying on the hood of a patrol car.) She shot at the intruder; I don't know if he was hit….Can someone get that shoe away from the dog? It's evidence."

Hoot told Jake to get the shoe. No one else dared to try.

The conversation continued until Hoot realized that he had all of the information possessed by the detective. Hoot took to flirting, "We need to quit meeting like this. Let's get together for a drink sometime." Tim noticed for the first time that the detective was slim, fit and actually quite attractive, if maybe a little young and tall for Hoot.

"I'd like that," replied the detective as she gave Hoot a card with her cell phone number.

Jake, Jen, their daughter Eloise, Tim, Hoot and Princess all sat in the big den in the rear of the house overlooking the swimming pool. The pool was now lit up. The whole house was lit up. Hoot noticed that Princess had specs of what appeared to be blood in her muzzle. He started to say: *What an ugly dog,* but stopped in time. *Don't say anything bad about a man's dog or child,* he reminded himself. Jen produced a wash cloth from the kitchen, lovingly wiped the dog's face, and gave her a dog biscuit which she ate in one bite.

Tim spoke for the first time all night. "What happened?"

Jen was surprisingly calm. "I was watching TV back here when the doorbell rang. I was really into some stupid show and never even gave it a thought. Eloise and Princess were resting and watching some other show upstairs with her door closed. I open the door and this little Mexican looking man asks for Jake. I didn't answer, and when I tried to close the door, he reached in and grabbed my arm. I yelled at him to let me go. The next thing I know he is trying to drag me out of the house."

Eloise chimed in. "I heard the commotion. Princess was already pawing at my door, and as I opened the door, she was down the stairs before I could take a step. The next thing I hear is blood curdling cries from a man's voice and then gunfire. I arrived downstairs just in time to see a small silver sedan flying off down the street."

Jen had listened without interrupting. She continued, "The man had my arm and was reaching for his gun when Princess barreled into him like a linebacker; only this linebacker was biting and tearing at the man with a fierceness that startled me. The man dropped his gun. The gun was just sitting there on the front steps, so I picked it up and tried to shoot him, but I couldn't because Princess was all over him. He eventually pulled loose and ran for his car. Princess grabbed his heel and he just got away by slipping out of the shoe. As soon as he was away from Princess, I started shooting."

Everyone was mesmerized by the telling. Hoot spoke first. "Did you hit him?"

Jen was now visibly upset. Princess jumped up on the couch and put her head in Jen's lap. "I don't think so. I did hit the car because I heard the window shatter as he jumped in and sped off."

Hoot asked for clarification. "Are you sure that the man never tried to come in?"

Jen did not hesitate. "No, he was trying to take me with him, of that I am certain."

Hoot shook his head. "Big D's partner, I will talk to Jubilee. You had better get out of town."

Jen did not flinch. "I am not going anywhere until Eloise is properly married." She left no room for argument.

Jake spoke. "I'll hire some men to protect Jen and Eloise. Princess will stay with them full time as well."

Tim, turned to Hoot, "Will that cute detective let you know if they catch anyone?"

Hoot smiled. "I'll see that she keeps me informed. There will be drive-bys from the patrol officers until she calls them off."

At 5:00 am the next morning, Buddy and Jake sat drinking coffee in Buddy's shop. Jake had been up all night with Princess at his feet and a shotgun in his lap. A private detective employed by Hoot had relieved Jake at 4:30 am.

"Buddy, I am in trouble again." Jake told Buddy the whole story.

As usual Buddy was unfazed. "I'll call the Ebarb brothers. They will see to it that nothing happens to Jen or Eloise."

The Ebarbs, also known as Big Ax and Little Ax, owed something to Buddy. They must have, because in spite of their successful masonry business, they were always available when Buddy called. It was odd to some that Little Ax was six inches taller than Big Ax and several years younger. Big Ax was thought to be meaner, but some argued that Little Ax was either meaner or at least more dangerous because of his pleasant personality. It sounds like a cliché, but it was the truth: no one messed with the Ebarb brothers twice, no matter how drunk or drugged they might have been. It was the Ebarb camp that the FBI had searched with Pinky. It was the DeSoto Parish Sheriff's Office who had been afraid to set foot on their property.

Buddy called. "Big Ax can you do me a favor? You will be paid."

Big Ax did not hesitate. "Sure what do you need?"

"Jeannette Cane needs protection. Can you help me? I think we will need your brother. You will need to watch her daughter too. Can you stay with them for a couple of weeks?"

The Ebarbs were happy to guard Jen; they liked her and she liked them. Jen came to realize that Big Ax reminded her of her father when he had been younger. The fact that she was beautiful as was her daughter, combined with staying in a million dollar house made it even more appealing.

Big Ax replied, "Little Ax can be there this morning. I will need to see to it that my jobs are covered. I can be there by six tomorrow night."

The Ebarbs moved in with Jake and Jen and would stay until the wedding. The Canes would be safe. After the wedding, Jake was planning to disappear with Jen to somewhere,though he didn't know exactly where.

CHAPTER 23. *DUST ON THE BIBLE.*
Kitty Wells, written by Johnny and Walter Bailes

https://www.youtube.com/watch?v=TEbP5hgK4Yc

There are few people with the intuition of Harry Earl "Hoot" Pruett. Somehow Hoot knew that Jubilee had a role in the events at the Cane's house. The next morning Hoot was on a plane to Memphis. He needed to be with Jubilee when he confronted him. He did not know what Jubilee would say, but he could learn much from his demeanor…information he could never obtain in a phone call.

Hoot arrived with no appointment. Hoot knew that he was onto something when Jubilee ended a meeting with his staff and allowed him into his office. Hoot spoke first. "Jubilee, you know why I am here." It was not a question.

Jubilee seemed to ignore the statement and started in on what first appeared to be a totally random thought. "Hoot, you and I are competitive men. We like to win. I bet you don't like to be passed on the interstate, do you? We want to be first."

Jubilee appeared to slightly hang his head. "Have you ever put winning above all else?" Hoot did not respond, Jubilee continued, "I 'always get my man.' You might not be shocked to hear that the reputation is a curse. When you have continued success, people expect continued success. Do you understand what I am saying?"

Hoot did understand. He also had the weight of a reputation, one that was difficult to live up to.

"Hoot, I fear… I know that I am the cause of what happened last night. I wanted to win. I was at a dead end. I did not consider the consequences of my actions."

Hoot's hunch had brought him to Jubilee's office, but he was confounded by this outpouring. He knew better than to say anything that might stem the flow. He just quietly nodded assent and waited for Jubilee to continue.

Jubilee knew that Jake had the money, and he knew that Hoot was not going to divulge anything, yet he kept talking. "The men who accosted Mrs. Cane are employees of Cortez Castaneda. Castaneda staked Big D with some of the money he used in the attempt to buy the drugs from Kelley. I arranged for Castaneda to learn that Jake has the money."

Hoot just nodded.

"I have a tape where Castaneda claims to have given Big D money, but I don't see how that alone will support a conviction. A lawyer like you will punch insurmountable holes in any case I try to bring." Jubilee was quiet, waiting for a response from Hoot.

"You're not giving up, you can't. Who do you want more? Jake or Castaneda?"

Jubilee did not hesitate. "Castaneda- can you help me get him?"

Hoot would keep his cards close to the vest. He would reveal nothing. "How can I do anything?"

"I'm not sure. Are the Canes safe?"

Hoot could answer that question. "Jeannette and her daughter are being protected by the Ebarb brothers; they're safe. Jake is playing cowboy. Thinks he is protecting himself. Maybe a death wish."

Jubilee was thinking out loud. "They won't kill him until they get the money. Do you think they know that Buddy, and not Jake, has the money?"

Hoot was thinking, but not out loud. *How could he? I don't know that myself. How does Jubilee know? It does make sense.*

Jubilee was on a roll. "I doubt they know anything about Buddy."

Hoot piped in. "Any deal we make will involve total immunity, no exceptions, for Jake, Jeanette, Buddy, and the Ebarb brothers, with judicial approval for crimes known and unknown in Federal Court and in the courts of both states."

Now it was Jubilee who was a little flustered. "What crime has Jeannette committed? For that matter, what crimes have the Ebarb brothers committed?"

"Jubilee, I never said that anyone committed any crimes. In fact, none of the people I mentioned are guilty of anything. If you took my request to indicate

otherwise, you are mistaken. You and I both know that
there are obscure federal crimes that can jump up and
bite poor unsuspecting people in the ass. Any deal we
make will include future actions by those people
mentioned, at least until this matter is closed. I am not
going to subject my client to prosecution for crimes
allegedly committed in an effort to help you convict
Castaneda or anyone else."

Jubilee acted like his feelings were hurt. "Hoot,
you don't trust me?"

"Jubilee, I don't trust anyone. That's not my
job. I trust no one. Don't put on that hurt feeling
bullshit with me. Any deal we make will be supported
by an ironclad agreement drawn up by Jake's silk
stocking lawyer and Tim. I will take no chances. You
have nothing with which to convict my client. The only
reason we are talking is because my client needs your
help to stay alive."

Jubilee dropped the hurt feelings charade. "Let
me see what I can do. I pray that your client lives long
enough for me to put this all together."

Hoot once again broke his sacred rule by writing his cell phone number on the back of his business card and handing it to Jubilee. "We better move fast. There is no telling what Castaneda might do."

Jubilee silently agreed. The man had an army of desperate illegal aliens. *There is indeed "no telling what he might do."*

CHAPTER 24. *A FOOL SUCH AS I.*
Hank Snow

https://www.youtube.com/watch?v=qtJz_Wm-gG0

Preparations for the *Wedding of the Century* continued as well as could be expected. By virtue of being there, the Ebarb brothers found themselves in the middle of the preparations. Jen either shamed or cajoled both brothers to trim their hair and beards and to put away their biker attire. The change clearly made the wedding planner, florist, and preacher more comfortable, if not the brothers.

The Municipal Auditorium is a big place, and Jen was determined to fill it up. She ignored the fact that she was competing with several other large weddings on the same night. Everyone who was anyone in Shreveport and half of Dallas, on the groom's side, were invited. Jen loved every minute. Eloise, at her father's insistence, went along with her mother as quietly as she could.

"You did what?" It was the day before the wedding, and Jake and Jen were sitting at the breakfast bar alone. Jen could not believe what Jake had said. "Tell me you are kidding."

Jake was unapologetic. "You heard me. I want them here where I can keep an eye on them. Don't worry. I seriously doubt they will come."

Jen was livid. "Jake, tell me that you did not invite Kelley and his girlfriend and Jubilee Jones to Eloise's wedding."

"Don't worry. Kelley won't come and Jubilee, or at least some of his agents will be there anyway. Hell Jen, with as many people as you have invited, it won't be possible to see everyone. If they do come, you'll never see them."

"Yeah, right. I won't notice two black people in a sea of white." Jen had a point.

Jake was acting like a drunken redneck. "Well it's done. I am not calling them and telling them not to come. You've got plenty of other things to worry about."

Jen had to agree with the last statement. "They better not come, and, if they do, they better not make a scene."

Jake did not know why he had sent the invitations. He just felt like it was the thing to do. Something compelled him, all the time knowing that Jen would object, so he never asked. "I'll see to it that there are no problems."

At that same instant, Kelley and Jackie sat drinking coffee at his Memphis townhouse. They had already packed for Shreveport at Jackie's insistence. They would leave after breakfast. When Jackie saw her name in calligraphy on the engraved invitation she was hooked, she was going. Kelley had no choice. "Explain again who these Canes are?"

"I told you Jackie, he is a business associate. I don't even know her, and I don't know the girl that's getting married." Jackie had so badly wanted to see this wedding that Kelley had finally agreed to go. That and his hope that the invitation was a sign that Jake had come up with a means by which he could transfer the money. He bought Jackie a new pale yellow dress with black patent leather heels for the occasion. She would turn heads. Kelley wondered if they should tone down the outfit until he recognized that Jackie would be one of only a few blacks in attendance, and they would likely be the only mixed couple. Heads would turn no matter what she wore.

Jackie had her doubts about the association between Kelley and the Canes. As far as she could tell, Kelley did not own any stocks. Why would he be in business with a stockbroker? Yet, Jackie was filled with curiosity, anticipation, and a feeling of unshakeable trepidation, somehow compelled to go to the wedding for reasons she did not understand.

Another unlikely guest had already left Memphis for Shreveport. Jubilee had other reasons to attend. It had been weeks since the attack on Jen, and the FBI had reassigned the people who had been keeping tabs on the Canes. Like Jackie, Jubilee had this feeling deep in his gut that he should attend the wedding. Unlike Jackie, he knew the basis for his impulse. Jubilee was working on a deal with Hoot, but

there had been pushback from several fronts. Jubilee
did not have a deal and was not certain that he ever
would. Jubilee had a feeling that there just might be
trouble waiting for him in Shreveport. As he drove
through Arkansas, he hoped his hunch was wrong,
wrong just this once.

From the south on I-49 another unwanted and
uninvited guest was headed north toward Shreveport.
Cortez was not alone. He was accompanied by his two
best men, or rather, the two best men he had left. Cortez
did not consider himself to be a man of intuition and
hunches. No Cortez thought himself to be a calculating
man, a thoughtful man, not a man who acted on
impulse. In the last few months, four of his men had
disappeared and one had returned chewed up like a dog
toy. Cortez had thought it through, and he was
convinced that he was on the right track, a track that
would lead him to the missing money. He was
convinced of another thing: James Cane was not what
he appeared to be. No, James Cane, while appearing to
be an upstanding citizen and husband, was actually a
dangerous criminal capable of anything. A man who

had likely, orchestrated the killing field in Brownsville; a man who had killed Big D, and a man who had probably killed others, including several of Cortez's own employees.

As he rode in the back of a white two-year-old Ford Explorer, Cortez was planning his next move. He would be careful, but he would get what was his. Scouts had preceded Cortez, and they were in place. Yes, a plan was coming together. The only person who did not have a feeling of impending doom or disaster was the target, James Caldwell "Jake" Cane.

CHAPTER 25. *HONKY TONK MAN.* Johnny Horton, written with Tillman Franks

https://www.youtube.com/watch?v=Dh6WaV2qLGI

The Canes met John the *Sperm Donor's* parents for the first time in person at the rehearsal dinner. Jake had specific instructions from Jen "Quit calling him by that name-- now." The parents were members of a club in Dallas with reciprocal privileges at the University Club. Even with that connection Jake was forced to call in a few favors and to grease a few palms in order to obtain a room on such short notice. In the process, Jen reminded Jake of a universal truth: *"if a problem can be solved with money, it's not really a problem."* Jake took the advice without comment but was thinking, *Jen seems to have forgotten the time when there was no money with which to solve problems.*

John's father and grandfather were both prominent members of the Dallas medical community; the father an ophthalmologist and the grandfather a general surgeon. Jake's mother, the first Eloise, was in her element. These were her people. Jake likewise did fine. Many of his clients were doctors, and he knew what to say and what to keep to himself. Such as, *why can't you bunch of doctors teach your descendant about birth control?* Jen also did fine. As it turned out, John's mother grew up in a middle class family in Port Arthur, Texas, and was working in the business office of Baylor Hospital when she met John's father.

The party was a success and might have been a huge success if not for the fact that Jake suddenly became falling down, word-slurring drunk. Jen would later learn that the near disaster was caused by a combination of alcohol and some "mood-altering" drugs Jake had obtained from his doctor. A scene was just barely averted when Jen realized the predicament and had Big Ax escort Jake out of the club. Jake had failed to mention the drugs to Jen and had failed to read the precautions clearly written in the several pages of imperceptivity small print that accompanied the prescription.

With apologies, Eloise's brother was forced to give his father's toast. John the future doctor and erstwhile sperm donor, could only just contain his glee over Jake's behavior. As he whispered and snickered to Eloise, "What goes around comes around," Eloise ignored her husband to be. She was neither amused by him nor by her father. John's family wondered to each other about the presence of the Ebarb brothers. Even dressed up and coiffured by Jake's barber they still looked and acted out of place. Instead of joining the party they seemed to be spending all of their time watching the servants and people who were not part of the wedding party. The explanation: *black sheep cousins, every family has them, right?*

Jen now realized why Jake had remained so calm; in the midst of planning a rushed wedding, and even in the face of the fact that the Canes were now unwilling prey for a gang of hoodlums. Hoodlums who were probably willing to kill to get what they wanted. Jake was calm, drugged, but calm.

There was more to the story that Jen did not know. Jen thought that the "authorities" were in on the deal and busy protecting Jen and her family. In fact, the only protection being afforded to the Canes was from the Ebarbs and through an occasional drive-by from the local police. Jubilee wanted and had requested protection, but with no support from Senator Davis, Jubilee was being thwarted in his efforts by the bureaucracy of the law enforcement agencies of two states and the federal government.

As is often the case with bureaucrats, a decision can get them in trouble while no decision seldom will. The wheels were grinding frustratingly slow for Jubilee. All the while Jen and especially Jake were basking blissfully in their ignorance. Jen more because of her focus on the wedding and Jake through his newly acquired fitness, study of self-defense, and the marvels of modern chemistry.

The Explorer parked on the north side of Travis Street containing three Hispanics caught the attention of Big Ax as he steered Jake to the Ford Police Interceptor parked in the garage across from the American Tower. By the time Jake was loaded into the back seat and being driven from the garage, the Explorer was gone. After the party, Little Ax drove the remaining Canes safely home, crowded into Jen's Lexus SUV.

Big Ax gave the license plate from the Explorer to Buddy. It was registered to a Mike Smith in Mamou, Louisiana. Carlos was too smart to be driving a vehicle that could be traced back to him. For his part Jake slept like a rock and woke up with a splitting headache and an angry wife. Jen did not need to convince Jake that he should throw away the pills and stay away from alcohol. He would take no chances on his daughter's wedding day.

CHAPTER 26. *COCA COLA COWBOY.*
Mel Tillis

https://www.youtube.com/watch?v=xdVLEo3JyWc

It can be downright beautiful in Shreveport on some fall days. The wedding day was one of those days, bright sunshine, temperatures in the mid-60's, and uncharacteristically low humidity. The stars were aligning for John and Eloise. Actually, Eloise and especially John would have rather gotten married in the judge's office and gone off somewhere alone. In truth, the stars were aligning for Jen, who was now going to have the wedding she had been denied over twenty years ago.

It was, by all accounts, a beautiful wedding, and Eloise literally glowed, amid the whispers that the glow was caused by her pregnancy. Shreveport is a small town not known for keeping secrets. Nonetheless, there was no denying her beauty, nor the beauty of the mother of the bride, who wore a flowing cream colored dress which, some commented, did not accent Jen's

figure. The reason of the loose fitting was the one secret
that would be kept for a few more months.

Finding a band for the wedding had proven to
be impossible until, at the last minute, one of the other
weddings cancelled. Rumor has it, the potential groom
had too much fun at his bachelor party. The late
cancellation was good for two reasons, a band was now
available and many guests who were otherwise torn
between which of the weddings to attend would now
free to attend Jen's extravaganza. Furthermore, no
more had been seen of the Hispanics or of the white
Ford Explorer. The stars were indeed aligning.

As if it could not get any better, Jake learned
that the band included in its repertoire several classic
country songs, and Jake had surreptitiously slipped
them a bribe in return for their promise to play a few of
those songs and the promise to keep the bribe from Jen
and Eloise. Jen might not have objected. After all, the
theme of the wedding was the Louisiana Hayride. Jen
choose that theme for two reasons. One spoken and a
second reason that she kept to herself.

The official spoken motivation for the theme
was to highlight the fact that the venue for the wedding

was the same venue that had hosted the Hayride over fifty years earlier, a way of subtly explaining the poor condition of the place and to make it an asset. *Can you believe that Hank Williams and Elvis actually performed in this room?* The unspoken purpose for the theme was to placate Jake. With the Hayride as the theme, she would get no complaints from Jake about the costs, especially the costs of decorations.

As it turned out, the auditorium had changed little in fifty-plus years and, if anything, the place looked better for Jen's efforts than it ever had during the heyday of the Hayride. Guests would need and did overlook for the most part the condition of the bathrooms. The many open bars helped in that regard.

It was Little Ax that first became suspicious of the muscular Hispanic who was serving the wedding party as they waited in one of the dressing rooms for their entrance into the reception. There seemed to be a bulge under his black waistcoat near his left arm pit. Little Ax quietly followed the man until they were adjacent to an outside door. With one quick move the man found himself in the alley behind the auditorium with his right hand pinned against his shoulder blade.

When Little Ax found that the bulge under the man's left arm was definitely a gun, the man was in an instant lying unconscious on the loose gravel and asphalt in the alley.

As luck would have it, the van for the band was nearby and open. Bad luck for the Hispanic as Little Ax spied a roll of duct tape in the van, which he expertly used to muffle and secure the man. A few minutes later the poor fellow awoke immobile among the trash of a rather large garbage dumpster.

Big Ax had seen his brother follow the waiter out of the dressing room. When Little Ax returned, he asked , "What's with that guy? He looks out of place to me."

The Ebarb brothers are not what anyone would call big conversationalists. Little Ax replied. "Never talked to him but he was whining in Spanish before I knocked him out. He was carrying this gun." Little Ax showed his brother the gun he now had in the side pocket of the blazer Jen had bought him from Pope's. "According to his ID, he lives in Lafayette."

Big Ax wanted more information. "Where is he now? Was anyone with him? Did anyone see you?"

Little Ax answered in as few words as was possible. "He's in the dumpster. Not that I saw. No one saw me."

Big Ax was thinking. "I thought those guys in the Explorer last night were up to something. Did you notice the Mexican limo driver?"

The Ebarbs had not ridden from the church in the limo. They had come in Jen's Lexus with the plan of taking the Canes home after the reception. Little Ax answered his older brother. "Yes I did. He also looked out of place. He won't be driving any Canes again tonight."

Big Ax continued, "We can protect the girls, but we may need help with the 'cowboy.'" They had taken to calling Jake by that name in light of his behavior on the prescription drugs. "Is Buddy coming?"

"I doubt it. He has never been much for this type of thing," replied Little Ax.

Big Ax cut his eyes to the wedding party. "Me neither, but have you noticed some of these bridesmaids? I could put on this monkey suit for some of that."

The wedding party was leaving to make their entrance into the reception. Big Ax was now serious, "You stay focused on Jen, and I'll watch Eloise. Call Buddy, see if he answers. Until Buddy gets here, the cowboy is on his own."

The band announced the entrance of the wedding party and everyone did their obligatory dances. Jake was almost in tears when he learned that the newlyweds choose *Hey Good Lookin'* for their first dance. Jake had always considered the song to be their song, Jen and Jake's song.

The song he and Eloise danced to was just vaguely familiar to Jake. He had heard it before, but could live without ever hearing it again. As these thoughts passed through his mind, he realized that he was getting old. His dad had had the same feelings about Rod Stewart and the Eagles and every other popular band of Jake's youth. When it came time for Jake and Jen to dance, the band played *Almost*

Persuaded, just as Jake had instructed. The band lacked a tenor who could come close to matching David Houston's range, so one of the girls sang the song. Tears welled in Jen's eyes, as she whispered in Jake's ear, "I will forgive you."

Jake responded, "It will never happen again."

Jen did not respond, but it was clear what she was thinking. *It better not happen again.*

Jake was wishing that the song could go on forever. The band followed *Almost Persuaded* with *Jambalaya,* and all of the dancers in the crowd now joined in. Jake and Jen were separated in the crowd when one of the waiters approached Jake. "There is a problem out front. Can you go out and talk to the guard?" The city had required that off-duty police be hired as security. Jake did not want to leave, but duty called and he did.

CHAPTER 27. *YESTERDAY'S WINE.*
George Jones, with Merle Haggard

https://www.youtube.com/watch?v=5IsWBHy-d5M

It should not surprise anyone that Jubilee Jones was able to blend into the crowd at the reception. He attracted several people who wanted to meet and talk to him, mostly politicians well aware of the fact that half of all voters in Caddo Parish are black. If this black man warranted an invite to this wedding, he must be important. *Why don't I know him,* was most likely the thought process. Jubilee had always enjoyed people, could talk to anyone and relished the attention.

Hoot saw Jubilee and made a point of saying hello. "Jubilee, I didn't expect to see you here. Please meet Dale; she is also in law enforcement." Hoot had brought as his date the detective who was investigating the incident involving Jen a few weeks earlier. "How's our deal progressing?"

"Hoot, not so well, some of my superiors are not anxious to make a deal, while the murder of two state troopers remains unsolved. What a great party. It is not every day that I attend a soiree like this." Hoot spied one of the judges. Hoot was obliged to speak to the judge who was at that moment alone. As Hoot walked away, one of the waiters, a Hispanic looking man, approached Jubilee and whispered something in his ear.

Cortez Castaneda also moved easily through the crowd with a woman he had rented and dressed for the night. Cortez wore a grey suit, a muted maroon tie, and black wingtip shoes. His dark hair was no longer slicked back; he looked like a banker who had just left the Shreveport Club. He even told those whom he met that he was a banker from New York. The rented girl was also understated with light brown hair and a light brown dress. The only thing incongruous about her appearance was her eye makeup. If she had applied any more eye makeup, it is doubtful she could have opened her eyes. She was instructed to say nothing. Cortez saw Jubilee from a distance and instinctively made certain that he stayed far enough away from Jubilee so as not to be seen. It was too much of a coincidence for this black man, Cortez now recognized as a cop, to be in a bar with Danielle Stephens in Memphis and also at this wedding.

One couple did stand out, Kelley and Jackie. Kelley wore a tailored dark blue suit that perfectly fit his athletically toned body and Jackie in the pale yellow dress that accented her figure and contrasted flawlessly with her ebony skin. They made a stunning couple, clearly in the wrong place, attractive, but not particularly approachable. Kelley was decidedly uncomfortable, but hid it well. Jackie was too interested in everything to be uncomfortable. Jackie had worked similar events in New Orleans and was absolutely enjoying the view from the other side of the server line.

One of the servers approached Jackie, "Keishonda, what are you doing here?"

Keishonda was Jackie's real name. It was Kelley who first called her Jackie. The server and Jackie hugged. "Lakeisha, how are you?" Jackie did not need to ask what Lakeisha was doing; they had worked similar events together in New Orleans. Lakeisha was a Katrina refugee; Jackie knew, she didn't need to ask.

Jackie ignored the question. How could she explain when she didn't know the answer herself. "Meet my friend Kelley. Can you believe it?"

Lakeisha could not believe it. She wondered to herself, *did she get hit in the head during Katrina?* Just then the head server motioned for Lakeisha. She had to go. "My sister Laquita is here, too. She is in the back. I will get her to come by and see you. We need to talk. Will you be here tomorrow?"

Jackie did want to see her old friends. "Yes, we are staying at the Horseshoe. Ask for Ronald Kelley. Please tell Laquita to come find me. Tell her that I have on a yellow dress." They both laughed, Jackie would not be hard to find.

A few minutes later Laquita came from the back. Jackie could tell that she had more to say than just hello. "Jackie, do you know that pleasant black man who was standing over there?" Laquita was motioning to the area where Jubilee had been earlier.

Jackie looked for Jubilee. He was no longer where he had been standing a few minutes before. "No-- hello how are you?" Laquita's demeanor told Jackie that her question was more important. "Yes, he is an FBI agent. Why do you ask?"

"Keishonda, you know how people think of us as furniture? You know how they talk in front of us as if we aren't even there?"

Jackie was not that far removed from her days as a server. "I sure do. It has always amazed me."

Laquita intuitively knew that Kelley was some kind of cop. She spoke to both of them. "I overheard two men talking. They are going to take the black guy and the father of the bride and throw them off of the Neon Bridge if they don't get something. I didn't hear what they want."

Kelley looked toward the front door, in time to see Jake leaving the building. Jake was alone. Jubilee was nowhere in sight.

CHAPTER 28. *JAMBALAYA (ON THE BAYOU)*. Hank Williams

https://www.youtube.com/watch?v=Yog-cNfqnig

The Municipal Auditorium is no longer in the best part of town. Perhaps that explains why it is not used as often as one might expect. Cortez had no problem in creating a diversion for the security officers. Jubilee had been told that an officer wanted to talk to him, but no police officer was in front of the building when Jubilee came out. All three officers were off chasing several boys who seemed to be breaking into the fancy cars and SUVs in the parking lot.

A Hispanic man standing next to a long black Lincoln limousine and dressed in the uniform of a limousine driver spoke to Jubilee. "My boss wants to know if you are from Memphis?"

Jubilee answered without hesitation. "I am. What can I do for you?"

The man motioned toward the back seat of the Limo. "He wants to talk to you."

There wasn't any obvious reason for Jubilee to
be suspicious, he should have been, but the enjoyment
of the party had caused him to let down his guard.
There had been no sign of trouble at the wedding or at
the reception, and Jubilee was relaxed. Jubilee poked
his head into the limo and found himself confronted by
another man, this one clearly Hispanic pointing a gun in
his face. The man behind Jubilee spoke. "Put your
hands on the seat in front of you."

Jubilee felt another gun poking him in the back
just above his belt. The man behind him quickly
removed Jubilee's revolver and shoved him into the
limo. Minutes later, Jake received the same treatment
except Jake wasn't carrying a weapon. Jake and Jubilee
were instructed to sit with their backs toward the front.
The men were now joined by Cortez who sat in the
back of the limo facing them.

Jubilee now recognized Cortez. He didn't look
at all like the man Jubilee had seen in the bar in
Memphis, but it was Cortez, no doubt. As Jubilee
studied the face, he recognized that he had seen this
man at the reception, (Cortez had skipped the wedding)
but had not realized who he was. That revelation

alarmed Jubilee. In his younger days he would have identified Cortez at the wedding, of that he was certain. Cortez would have never gotten this far. Jubilee spoke. "Can you tell me what this is all about?"

By now the man in the uniform had taken the driver's seat and was slowly pulling away from the auditorium. The driver had given Cortez Jubilee's wallet. "FBI, I'm impressed. I've never killed an FBI agent. I don't forget a face, especially when it is somewhere it should not be. I saw you in a bar in Memphis a few weeks ago. Why were you in that bar?" The coincidence of seeing this same man at the wedding was too much for Cortez to brush off.

Jubilee answered wanting to keep Cortez talking while he found some way out of the car. "I live in Memphis. You must know that this place is swarming with FBI."

If Cortez was concerned by the bluff, he didn't show it. "You are the only person I have seen who even remotely resembles an FBI agent. Why would the FBI be at this wedding?"

"I am not at liberty to disclose that information." Before Jubilee had completed the sentence he regretted the words. *Where did that ridiculous statement come from?*

Cortez was likewise unimpressed. "Don't give me a bunch of your bullshit. You're here for the same reason I am." Cortez now shifted his focus to Jake. "To see this little turd. I don't know what you are investigating about him, exactly, but I know he is the reason you are here."

Cortez continued. "This asshole is not as he appears, but you already know that. He killed a bunch of people up in Tennessee and took my money and my drugs. He has since murdered Big D and several of his men and has more recently killed several of my employees. He has my money and my drugs, and I intend to get them back."

Jake started to say something but Jubilee spoke first. "If all you say is true, you have answered your own question. That's exactly why the FBI is at this wedding."

The limo was now stopped behind the First Methodist Church, which is less than half of a mile from the Auditorium, the same church where the wedding had taken place less than an hour earlier.

Jake spoke this time, more babble than coherence. "You've got me all wrong. Where did you come up with such a crazy story? I am not the man you are after. I need to get back to the wedding. My wife will be looking for me."

Cortez just smiled. "Your wife will be joining us shortly. I have two men working as waiters who will be here with your wife very soon. In fact they should already be here." Then he addressed the driver. "Did you see Ricky and Manuel before we left?"

The driver replied. "I saw Ricky, when he talked to these two. I did not see Manuel. I haven't seen Manuel for a while."

As this conversation was taking place, Ricky was lying unconscious next to a large trash bin behind the Auditorium. The impression his head had left in the side of the trash bin could be seen above his bloodied, limp body. Big Ax was at that very moment busy wrapping him in the remainder of the duct tape. If Ricky awoke, he would find himself in the dumpster among the trash, with the missing Manuel as his only companion. Jen was looking for Jake, but she would not be joining Cortez's party.

Jubilee spoke again. "Who are you?" Jubilee knew the answer. What he really wanted to know was what Cortez had in mind.

Cortez wasn't worried about anyone knowing his name; he was not planning to leave any witnesses. He just didn't feel like answering any questions. "Tell me Mr. FBI agent, where has the little turd hid my money and my stash?"

Jubilee responded. "I am afraid that I don't know what you are talking about," wishing he had never said anything about the swarm of FBI agents. "I am just in Shreveport to attend the wedding of my friend's daughter."

Cortez now motioned to the driver. "We have waited long enough. We will come back for the wife." Cortez then turned back to Jubilee. "We are going to take you to that neon bridge. We are going to hang you off the side of that bridge. If I don't get some answers, I will drop you." Then Cortez turned to Jake, "You will follow your friend, and if I don't get answers from you, your wife will be next."

Jubilee and Jake were each having the same thought at the same time. *I don't know where the money is and even if I did and even if I told him, there is no way he is going to let me live.*

CHAPTER 29. *HEART OVER MIND.*
Mel Tillis

https://www.youtube.com/watch?v=85vI4sZ8T4U

Kelley emerged from the Auditorium just in time to see the limo turning right onto Milam Street. He was not the cop he had once been, but he had to do something. Kelley was not from Shreveport, and he didn't know anything about the "Neon Bridge." To his left Kelley saw a familiar figure limping toward the Auditorium. Buddy had exhausted every excuse he could conjure up for missing the reception. He would make his appearance and be gone. Buddy and Kelley saw each other at the same time. Kelley spoke before Buddy could, "Do you know anything about a Neon Bridge?

Buddy did of course. "That's a crazy question." Buddy was now close enough to Kelley to see that it was an important if odd question. "Why do you ask?"

"Somebody has taken Jake and Jubilee and they are going to throw them off of the Neon Bridge."

Buddy's car, the old diesel Mercedes, was parked fifty yards away under a street light. "I know where it is," handing Kelley the keys to the Mercedes. "That old tan Mercedes is my car. Go get it and come pick me up. Pop the trunk when you get back."

Kelley had never been one to take instructions, but this time he did as told with no hesitation. The way Buddy was limping it made sense for Kelley to get the car and he was willing to bet that Buddy had items in his car that would prove helpful. Just then Buddy noticed Jackie. She had been standing by listening. Jackie asked Buddy, "What can I do?"

"You must be Kelley's girlfriend," Buddy thought and said aloud. "Go find the policemen and tell them to send an emergency detail to the Texas Street Bridge. Make sure they know that the people they find are likely armed."

Jackie could see an officer out in the parking lot. As Kelley drove up and popped the trunk, she was already heading toward the nearest cop.

The trunk slammed and Buddy eased into the passenger seat as quickly as he could. He was now carrying his Remington 700, fitted with a Leupold scope and a Viridian green laser. Buddy shouted out instructions as he loaded .308 Winchester shells into the rifle. "Turn this car around and take a left on Texas Avenue."

Had they continued straight ahead to Milam Street they might have seen the limo behind the church, but the quickest way to where Buddy was going was straight up Texas to Crockett and straight to the Clyde Fant Parkway. "Kelley do you remember where you met Jake by the river?"

Kelley did remember, but was not sure he knew how to get there or why Buddy was asking. "I remember. There are three bridges nearby. Is one of those bridges the Neon Bridge?"

Buddy reached into his glove box and pulled out Ruger 101, .38 special. "Yes, it's off to the north. If they are up there, we will be able to see them from the back of the Barnwell Center. Here take this." He said while handing Kelley the Ruger. "If you go up on the bridge you'll need this. I'll stay down on the bank and cover you. With this bum leg, I'd be no help in close quarters." Buddy was thinking ahead. Buddy always thought ahead.

When they reached the Barnwell parking lot, the bridge was lit up with neon lights but was otherwise nearly deserted. The limo was nowhere in sight. As Buddy struggled to get out of the car with his rifle, he saw the limo slowly drive to the middle of the bridge and stop. Buddy limped as fast as he could to the railing adjacent to the river. Kelley spoke, "What now?"

They just looked at one another without talking. The door on the back right side of the limo opened, and Jubilee could be seen being manhandled by a much younger, bigger, and stronger man.

Kelley's cop instincts kicked in. Kelley was a cop again, the cop he had once been. Kelley didn't wait for an answer. There was no time to waste. He put the big Mercedes in drive and headed for the bridge. If Kelley knew what he was going to do, he didn't share it with Buddy. Buddy turned his attention back to the bridge, to the limo, and to the man who was now holding a gun to Jubilee's head.

Up on the bridge, Jubilee was scared. It was looking for all the world like these criminals were going to do exactly what they said they would do, and no amount of talking by Jubilee had deterred them in the slightest. Jubilee was really wishing he had kept in better shape. His efforts to resist were proving fruitless. Then in the corner of his eye, he saw the Mercedes coming up the bridge. It seemed as though the Mercedes did not see the stopped limo. It was a moment later when Jubilee saw the flash of green light. He knew that light and immediately went totally limp, just before a bullet hit the man holding Jubilee squarely between his eyes.

Jubilee lay prone on the walkway of the bridge when he saw a big tan Mercedes Benz smash into the rear of the limo. It did not appear that it even tried to stop. Kelley jumped out of the Mercedes hollering. His tie was askew, his hair was in disarray, and he looked like another drunk going from one of the casinos to another. Kelley yelled at the limo, "Why the hell are you fools stopped in the middle of the bridge?"

With that the driver of the limo stepped out from the driver's seat brandishing an automatic weapon. He never got off a shot. Kelley shot him before he could raise his arm and twice more before he hit the pavement. At the same time Jake, having been thrown by the force of the collision into Cortez was wrestling Cortez for his gun. Unfortunately, Cortez was a much more skilled fighter and he quickly disengaged from Jake and promptly shot him twice. The first shot entered Jake just below his rib cage. The second shot glanced off of the left side of Jake's head rendering him unconscious.

Jake now laid in the back of the limo unconscious, bleeding profusely from the side of his head. He did not see Cortez shoot out the rear window of the limo and then quickly fire several shots one of which hit Kelley in the left thigh. In the confusion, Cortez had not seen what had happened to the man who had been ordered to throw Jubilee off of the bridge. Had Kelley not rammed the limo, Cortez would have known better than to exit the limo on its right side. With Kelley to the left of the limo, wounded, Cortez exited the limo on the right. He planned to use the limo as a shield as he finished off Kelly, who now lay bleeding in the road almost dead center of the bridge.

As Cortez exited the limo, he saw the body of his man lying lifelessly on the walkway. Next to him was Jubilee who was only capable of attempting to stay out of the line of fire. Unfortunately, for Cortez, before he could process what he was seeing, a rifle shot rang out from somewhere below and Cortez was dead.

Jubilee got to his feet and immediately went over to Kelley. A tourniquet of Jubilee's belt was quickly applied to Kelley's leg. Before the tourniquet was completely applied, a Shreveport police cruiser came racing up the bridge. Jubilee retrieved his ID, showed it to the patrolman and began barking out orders. "Lead me to the nearest trauma unit. I think the man in the back is dead and this man," motioning to Kelley "will be dead if we delay."

The officer was not leaving the scene. It was against policy. He would risk his job if he left the crime scene. Meanwhile, Jubilee had loaded Kelley into the back of the limo and was turning it around. He yelled at the officer, "Where is the nearest trauma unit?"

The officer was not budging; in front of him laid three men all of whom appeared to be dead. "What about these men?"

Jubilee replied impatiently. "They're in God's hands. There is nothing a man can do for them now."

Fate intervened, for just then a second unit arrived and the officer had his out. The officer yelled at the second unit before the officer could get out of his unit, "Lead this limo to LSU. There is a seriously injured person in the back."

In the back of the limo, Jake now began to bleed from his mouth. Kelley although himself in incredible pain found the strength to rip off his shirt and apply pressure to Jake's head wound. He could do nothing about the gut wound.

As police units continued to arrive on the bridge, now from both sides of the river, a non descript white work van stopped just south of the Barnwell Center. A man gingerly climbed in, the van slowly changed lanes, turned left on to Milam Street and disappeared from view.

CHAPTER 30. *JUST CAN'T LIVE THAT FAST (ANYMORE).* Lefty Frizzell

https://www.youtube.com/watch?v=IKd7nHHLCNU

The surgery on Kelley's leg was a success. He was going to fully recover. Jubilee's tourniquet had worked, saving him from bleeding to death. When he awoke from the anesthesia, Jackie was sitting by his bed, holding his free hand. Through the fog Kelley saw a face that displayed a combination of relief, love, and anger.

Jackie spoke directly. "Kelley, I will blissfully ignore a lot, but this has gone too far. I want some answers, and if I don't get them, you are going to need a new nurse. I want answers, or me and K J are gone." Jackie was pretty sure that she could get the answers on her own merit, but she was taking no chances so she played the K J card. She was certain that Kelley would do anything to keep K J in his life.

"Can this wait?" Kelley knew what was coming and wanted to put off this conversation for as long as was possible.

"No," was all she said.

Kelley could see that there was no way he was going to avoid the issue. "What do you need to know?" He intended to tell her as little as possible.

Jackie was not buying. "All of it, don't leave anything out."

Kelley hesitated, *all of it,* would be enough information to put Kelley in jail for the rest of his life.

Jackie sensed the dilemma. "Our relationship is at a crossroad. If you want to go forward you will need to show your trust in me."

Kelley did want to go forward, and, as his head cleared, it became evident to him that Jackie was perhaps the one person he could unquestionably trust. Jackie, put out a "No Visitors" sign, closed the door to the hospital room, and sat back down by Kelley's bed.

As it turned out, the telling didn't take all that long. After all, Jackie knew a good bit of it already from observation and a conversation she had earlier with Jubilee on Mud Island.

"So all of this is about dirty drug money?
Money that does not belong to you, money that has
caused nothing but misery and death."

Kelley did not answer.

Jackie continued. "This problem is solved for
us. The money is not yours and you will make no
further claim to it. We can live on what we earn and
keep our pride in the process." The manner in which
Jackie delivered the statement left no room for
argument.

"Okay," was Kelley's full response.

On another floor, the news was not as positive.
In fact, the only good news was that Jake had been
barely alive when the limo had arrived at the hospital.
The ER doctor, somewhat of a history buff with a lot of
education and little knowledge, remarked as they
removed Jake from the limo. "He is still alive. The
bullet looks like it entered his abdomen in the same
place where Huey Long was shot. See it exited his
back near his spine. Just like Huey Long." Jen had

arrived at the emergency room just in time to hear the comment.

Hours later Jake was still in surgery and none of the hospital personnel were saying anything. The assembled Canes were having an increasingly hard time interpreting no news as good news.

Jen cornered Buddy in the hall. "I have had all of this that I can take. Whatever happens to Jake, get rid of the money. Give it to the police. Give it to someone else, I don't care who. Just get rid of it."

"Okay," was Buddy's full response.

EPILOGUE.
TOGETHER AGAIN. James O'Gwynn

https://www.youtube.com/watch?v=7ooMC4JPbiI

A month later Jubilee Jones stopped by Buddy's shop. The Mercedes was repaired and looked better than it had on the wedding night. It was Tuesday evening; Buddy was alone in his shop drinking a beer. "Hello Agent Jones. Can I buy you a beer?"

"It's not Agent Jones anymore. I've retired. Thanks, I think I will."

Buddy retrieved a beer from the refrigerator in the shop. "What can I do for you?" Buddy was curious as to why he had not been visited by any detectives or FBI agents, but he was not about to ask.

Jubilee was his usual open self. "Oh nothing, I was just in town and wanted to come by and thank you."

Buddy took a sip from his beer. "For what?"

Jubilee reached out his hand. "For saving my life. Thank you."

Buddy shook Jubilee's hand but did not otherwise respond.

Jubilee spoke next. "By the way I closed the file on the Brownsville shooting before I retired. It seems that one Cortez Castaneda was responsible for the whole thing. You may have read that he died trying to kill me last month."

Buddy did not flinch. "I read about that in the paper. Did you know that Ronald Kelley was in my car when it happened? I guess he took it from the reception. I refused to press charges. I did not want any part of the legal system." Then changing the subject, "I am glad you are well. What are your plans?"

"We are moving back to New Orleans. I have taken a job with the Hilton Hotel. I will be in charge of security. You won't believe who I will be working with." Jubilee did not wait for an answer, "Ronald Kelley. Is that a coincidence, or what?"

They talked like old friends for over an hour, never again mentioning the now closed case. Jubilee reluctantly got up to leave. "Got to go. My wife is back at the hotel, and we are going to have a nice dinner. Going to the Anvil. I hear it's the best restaurant in town."

Buddy did not eat out often at such restaurants, but he had been there a several times. "It is good. Joe makes the best Old Fashioneds and meatballs in town. Try the chopped salad, it's outstanding."

Jubilee turned back to Buddy in the doorway. "By the way, did you hear that someone left a roller suitcase at St Jude's containing almost 1.3 million dollars? No one knows where the money came from."

"No Jubilee, I had not heard that. Come back and see me whenever you are in town. My door is always open to you."

Jen stood with Princess in the front yard of a blue shotgun house on Harmony Street in New Orleans's Garden District. Katrina was playing with K J in the front yard. Jen was now showing in her stylish maternity clothes. Princess growled at Katrina as Jen spoke to Jackie who was on the porch. "I want her to behave, but the pit-bull has a way of overriding the poodle. I'm going to put her back in the SUV."

Jackie looked contented. Married life and the return to her hometown was agreeing with her. "That's probably a good idea. Katrina can be protective. What do you think of the house?"

The house was a typical New Orleans shotgun. When Jen was young the house and the neighborhood would not have been desirable. Things were changing since the hurricane. The house was smaller than Kelley's Memphis Townhouse, but cost more. Jen would be polite; she grew up in an old house and now wanted new. "The house is adorable. I can't wait to see what you have done."

From the direction of the SUV Kelley was walking with Jake on his arm. Neither moved quickly. The women could see the new bond between the two. A strange, unlikely, inexplicable, bond. Jen spoke to Jake. "Will you hurry? We don't want to be late for our dinner reservation."

Jake replied in a weak voice. "I'm hurrying as fast as I can. If you wanted to get here earlier, we should have left earlier."

They all planned to dine at Commander's Palace where Jackie now worked.

Jen looked back to Jackie apologetically, "He is still weak and in pain. I almost lost the fool. I'll put up with him for a while longer."

Jackie nodded. "We must endure. They're all fools."

APPENDIX

I have now used over 90 songs from artists who performed at the Hayride in the three books that make up the *Cane's Landing* series. I predict that you have enjoyed many of these songs even if you have never been a country music fan. I want you to listen to them all. I hope you will at least try a few.

The first chapter in this book is titled: *Bloody Mary Morning* a song written and recorded by **Willie Nelson**. While Willie is probably one of the few active country music artist alive who could have actually appeared on the Hayride, he did not; at least during the time that it was a weekly program from 1948 to 1960. I have read that he did appear on one or more of the revival programs. The song was written in 1970, and recorded in 1973. It could have never been played on the original Hayride.

Chapter 2 is titled *He's a Good Ole Boy* by **Goldie Hill**. You may have never heard of Goldie Hill, but she was an early female country music star. Her recording of *I Let the Stars Get in My Eyes* went to number one on the country charts in 1953.

Chapter 3 is titled *Don't Mess with my Toot Toot* by **Doug Kershaw**. Doug was born in Cameron, Louisiana, and is one of the biggest Cajun stars. Born in 1936, he was just 24 when the Hayride ceased operations. He is still alive.

Chapter 4 is titled *Tiger Women* by **Claude King**, an artist who appeared on the Hayride and lived most of his life in Shreveport.

Chapter 5 is titled *Saginaw Michigan* by **Lefty Frizzell**. I changed the name of my character so that I could use this song.

Chapter 6 is titled *Heart over Mind* by **Mel Tillis**. This song was released long after the end of the Hayride. Mel is also still alive.

Chapter 7 is titled *I'm so Lonesome I Could Cry* by **Hank Williams**. Perhaps the greatest country artist, he rose to stardom while on the Hayride.

Chapter 8 is titled *She Thinks I Still Care* by **George Jones**, another giant of country music who performed on the Hayride.

Chapter 9 is titled *In the Jail House Now* by **Webb Pierce**, a member of the Country Music Hall of Fame and a regular on the Hayride. The song was a remake of an earlier hit by Jimmie Rogers.

Chapter 10 is titled Crystal *Chandelier* by **Carl Belew**. Belew, who began his singing career on the Hayride, had a hit with this song before Charley Pride.

Chapter 11 is titled *I'm Tired* by **Webb Pierce**.

Chapter 12 is titled *That's All Right* by **Elvis Presley**. This was one of the first songs Elvis sang on the Hayride.

Chapter 13 is titled *Cold Cold Heart* by **Hank Williams**.

Chapter 14 is titled *Big Mamou* by **Link Davis**. I could have chosen the version of this song that was recorded by Jimmy C. Newman. They both appeared on the Hayride. Jimmy was actually born in Mamou.

Chapter 15 is titled *Occasional Wife* by **Faron Young**. Faron is a Shreveport native, Fair Park graduate, and member of the country music hall of fame, who got his start on the Hayride.

Chapter 16 is titled *Louisiana Man* by **Doug & Rusty**. That would be Doug and Rusty Kershaw who both appeared on the Hayride. Rusty, the younger of the brothers, died in 2002.

Chapter 17 is titled *Invitation to the Blues* by **James O'Gwynn**. A great song also recorded by Ray Price, Roger Miller, Emmylou Harris, and Tom Waits.

Chapter 18 is titled *Walking the Dog* by **Webb Pierce**. This is the third Webb Pierce hit chosen as a chapter title for this book. I love Webb Pierce.

Chapter 19 is titled *Trouble's Back in Town* by the **Wilburn Brothers**. The Wilburn Brothers from Arkansas were among the first regulars on the Hayride appearing from 1948 to 1951.

Chapter 20 is titled *He'll Have to Go* by **Jim Reeves**. Jim Reeves was an announcer on the Hayride. He got his break as a singer when Hank Williams failed to show for a performance. How did Horace Logan fail to recognize his singing talent?

Chapter 21 is titled *Plastic Saddle* by **Nat Stuckey**. Stuckey was an announcer on KWKH radio station, which owned the Hayride. He appeared on the Hayride, but did not have any hits until after 1960.

Chapter 22 is titled *Jole Blon* by **Doug Kershaw, Jimmy C Newman and Joel Sonner**. This song is often referred to as the Cajun National Anthem. The English translation is "Pretty Blond." Every Cajun singer does a version of this song.

Chapter 23 is titled *Dust on the Bible* by **Kitty Wells**. This is a song written by Johnny and Walter Bailes who were members of the Bailes Brothers. They all appeared on the Hayride.

Chapter 24 is titled *A Fool Such as I* by **Hank Snow**. Horace Logan does not list Hank Snow as having appeared on the Hayride, but other sources report that he did. Having "Been Everywhere" I bet he did perform on the Hayride.   It's a great song. I had to include it; fools are a reoccurring theme in country music and in this book.

Chapter 25 is titled *Honky Tonk Man* by **Johnny Horton**. This song was written with Johnny's manager and bass player, Tillman Franks. Franks was a big influence in the careers of several country stars. Tilman was in the car when Johnny Horton was killed in east

Texas. He later managed and performed with David Houston.

Chapter 26 is titled *Coca Cola Cowboy* by **Mel Tillis**. Tillis will be 84 in August. He did not write this song, but is a prolific song writer who wrote too many hits to list here.

Chapter 27 is titled *Yesterday's Wine* by **George Jones and Merle Haggard**. Merle Haggard never performed on the Hayride.

Chapter 28 is titled *Jambalaya (On the Bayou)* by **Hank Williams**. Hank wrote the song. Most people think of it as a Cajun song, but it was written and originally recorded by a young man from Alabama. Hank's recording was number one for 14 weeks.

Chapter 29 is titled *Heart Over Mind* by **Mel Tillis**. This is the third Mel Tillis song, I must love him, too. This song was recorded by Ray Price before it was a hit for Mel Tillis.

Chapter 30 is titled *Just Can't Live That Fast Anymore* by **Lefty Frizzell**; a great talent who died too young.

The Epilogue is titled *Together Again* by **James O'Gwynn**; O'Gwynn's version of the Buck Owens classic.

If you have not listened to these tunes, it is not too late.

ACKNOWLEDGEMENTS

I again recognize Diane Turnley and Blake Martinez. Not only did they help proofread this book but they also each pointed out a separate problem with the plot. I thank my friend, Phil Nadeau, for providing me with a new character. Cortez Castaneda was Phil's idea. I am grateful to Danielle Fauber and Cindy Smith for their help and most of all for their patience and tact with an "old fool," and to Cathy Sledge for her proof reading and gentle editing. Finally, to my fans… thanks for waiting.

PATRICK HENNESSY

Patrick Hennessy was born in San Francisco, California, and grew up in Bossier City, Louisiana. Patrick graduated from Bossier High, Louisiana Tech and LSU Law School. He is a retired lawyer, having practiced law in Louisiana for many years.

Patrick now lives and writes in his home in the South Highlands area of Shreveport, Louisiana. He and his wife enjoy traveling and spending time at their shotgun house in uptown New Orleans.

59920400R00143

Made in the USA
Charleston, SC
18 August 2016